An Austrian March

Alyssa Hubbard

Copyright © 2014 Alyssa Hubbard

All rights reserved.

ISBN: 149216870X
ISBN-13: 978-1492168706

DEDICATION

I dedicate this work to my brother and my sister because I want to show them that you can achieve anything you set your mind to. Same goes to you reader. What is your dream?

CONTENTS

	Acknowledgments	i
1	The Sonata Form	1
2	The Fanfare	10
3	The First Strain	19
4	The Second Strain	30
5	The Dog Fight	39
6	The Trio	51
7	The Harmony	58
8	The Melody	67
9	The Finale	76
10	Epilogue	82
11	About the Author	85

ACKNOWLEDGMENTS

First off, thank you to my editor James Oliveri for his amazing work on this piece. His fine work has made my book a better book, and my skills as a writer even better. I can't thank him enough. I also want to thank my family for handling all of my stress with the patience of saints. You guys are the greatest. Thank you to my good friend Chelsea Rutledge for supporting me as both a reader and a friend. Your opinion is priceless to me. Finally, thank you to my readers for supporting my endeavors. Y'all are the reason I keep doing this, and I can't thank you enough.

1 – THE SONATA FORM

The world is a sheet of music, or at least that's how I see it. Everyone could see that if they took the time to notice, but of course that's easier said than done. Regardless, the world flows together, its people and their decisions creating notes and rhythms, all to create a harmonious tune.

But there are always accents. People change and grow. They add their own crescendos and staccatos, always different depending on the musician who decides to play the tune. The moods and tones create a distinctive piece, an individual path for the person to follow. No two musicians will ever play the part exactly the same, however, they can influence each other and intertwine their songs. But that's just how I see the world.

Perhaps it's due to my inclination as a musician. A bit obsessive, yes, but I like to think of it as one of my many quirks. Excuse me, I have yet to introduce myself. My name is Klemens Reinstadler, Austrian by birth and blood. I have an addictive personality where the arts are concerned, particularly with classical music, which I have found is seen as an oddity in America, where I am currently attending to my studies.

The music here is much different than what I know. The rock, pop, country, and all subsequent sub-genres that fall in between lack the quality I find in classical. There is no thought to any of it. It's all just raucous noise and synthesized beats, with hardly any rhyme or reason. And the lyrics? Laughable. It lacks principle, thought, and the basic passion that is required to make a long-lasting tune. They'll fade with time, but my classical will always remain.

While I don't care for the music, the institutions in America are fabulous, particularly that of my college - Julliard. The food is as good and much heartier than anything I had at home, though that could explain the immediate increase in my waistline. But I digress. Though America has its luxurious perks, the language itself lacks any creativity. With enough practice, one can create something beautiful, but the average language is far beyond artistic.

I gave up much of what I've always enjoyed to attend the wonderful university that is Julliard, but I would sacrifice nearly everything for my music. It has been my life from the beginning, but as time has gone by, I have noticed something lacking in my music that I hadn't before. I'm missing a particular emotion or feeling, perhaps? I can't be sure, as of yet, but my time here will be well spent. I won't leave until I find the missing step in my waltz, the lack of lilt in my Aria, my missing piece.

It's only a matter of time.

The speaker in our classroom, a dusty box, a cobweb-covered eyesore, crackled to life, and the sharp intake of breath at the other end had the entire room transfixed with curiosity.

"Klemens Reinstadler. Klemens Reinstadler, please come to the International Affairs Office."

I always fancied myself as someone who shied away from all kinds of attention, unless it involved a stage and an instrument beneath my fingers, of course. Otherwise, I kept to myself. That's not to say I would cow down in a public place. Oh no. My inner Austrian pride would never allow that. But I physically winced at the mention of my name over the speaker, and regretted it immediately as it drew the eyes from the speaker to me. No one ever used the speakers anymore. The school had expanded and technology made it much easier to just contact students directly, rather than interrupt an entire class, but not the International Student Affairs office. Most students who transferred from other countries had no cell phones or didn't speak English well enough to learn to use the American equivalent. It was much easier to teach them to come running if they heard their names over the speaker. Most would go quickly, but not me. I always hesitated.

But with the class at a pause and the teacher's stare making it obvious that I was the one to be called, I had no choice. Either I rose immediately or risked even further public humiliation. I rose from my seat, noting all the eyes trained on me as I disrupted the flow of the regular class day even further. I doubt that anyone knew me in that class. I knew most of their names, but I suppose that's just European courtesy. I tried my best to avoid the prying eyes, but the entire class, teacher included, lacked any decorum. I felt the rude stares even as I gathered my things and headed out of the classroom. Regardless of whether I'm watched or not, I consider myself an Austrian of the highest pedigree, and I carry myself as such.

As I walked down the hall, my riding boots clicking rhythmically, I found myself perturbed by the emptiness. I had only walked those halls when they were filled with other, buzzing students. But it was just me, and I had plenty of silence and room to think. It slowed my stride, but it wasn't often that I was able to daydream, and I reveled in it, even allowing my eyes to drift shut.

I found myself at the music hall, the one place in the world where I felt alive. The baby grand was already positioned at the center of the stage, and my hands were already placed on the chilling ivory. There was no music on the stand, but music wasn't necessary. I had memorized my favorite pieces, and I set to work on them immediately. A swift march, one that matched the rhythmic click of my boot heels on the tile floor. But the clicking eventually faded into the recesses of my mind, allowing the music to flow freely into every inch of my imaginary music hall. The fanfare sped up to a grand crescendo, the first strain imminent and pushing to be heard. I feared the notes would be botched, that the rhythm wouldn't be able to handle the impending finish of the fanfare and would subside into the lilt of the first strain. I was about to find out when something else began to intrude on my private performance.

It was a light tinkling, not unlike the sound of bells, and its beat disrupted the whole of my march. My fingers froze on the imaginary keys, the tinkling grabbing hold of my entire imaginary world. Even the clicking of my boots ceased, and I opened my eyes, surprised to find myself standing in front of the real music hall. The music hall, the one mine was fashioned after, was where the tinkling had come from. I listened for a few seconds before I realized that it was the baby grand piano. I had never heard it sound as unprofessional and amateur as it did while I stood out in the hall. My fingers twitched and I eyed the door. Surely whoever was in there wouldn't mind a bit of company and perhaps a few pointers. Plus, it would give me an excuse not to go the office. Austrians were punctual, but I could only take so much of the false cheeriness everyone in that office seemed to give off. Not to mention that they all spoke slowly and above average volume, as if every student who passed through their offices didn't understand them at a regular level. It was humiliating.

I shook the memories from my mind and the scowl from my face, then headed straight for the auditorium door. As slow and carefully as possible, I tried to open it, but the hinges squealed loudly. The sound had me gritting my teeth, but the tinkling kept on, uninterrupted. I let out a tense sigh, just enough to ease the nerves that had built up, then looked to the stage. The lighting had been altered. A spotlight was now centered on the stage where the piano stood. A pale silhouette hovered over the dark wood. The back drop was black, causing both the figure's clothes and the piano to bleed out. They looked like shadows, or perhaps even memories, especially with the added blue hue. It was angelic, and I longed to be a part of the scene.

But the tinkling continued to echo throughout the room and fell on my ears like a wave. It wasn't necessarily a terrible sound. I didn't think it was even possible to make a piano sound bad, but it certainly needed refinement. There was no order, yet the sounds seemed to carry a rhythm. I could feel the tremors in my hands starting up again, and I couldn't just stand there and listen for any longer. I cleared my throat, hoping the person would hear me and not be startled when I made my way to him. I couldn't be sure if he had heard me or not. The tinkling continued coming in waves as I made my way down the aisle.

Despite grazing several deep maroon chairs, which easily blended into the darkness of the seating area, I found the black steps to the stage. The lighting made it much harder to see, but it was all muscle memory by then. I had been in that hall both in my dreams and in everyday life. Practicing, performing, being, I basically lived in that hall, and by the time I made it onto the stage, I instinctively headed toward the piano. But there was already someone seated at the bench, his head dipped low as if resting it against the music stand. His fingers danced across the keys with no apparent control. With the element of surprise, I assumed, on my side, I took the chance to study the person. While I was much closer to him, it still seemed impossible to completely discern any key features.

He was nearly translucent. His clothes bled with the darkness, a black collared shirt and black jean-like pants, but his hair and skin bled into the light. It was an even more beautiful sight up close, and I had to wipe my eyes, just to be sure they weren't clouded. The most I could make out was that he was indeed male, and his hair was either blond or white. I assumed the former. If I had been a painter instead of a musician - perish the thought, though my brother would have been proud - my longing for a paintbrush would've been unbearable. It was as if I were watching an angel play, and the tinkling in the background made it seem even more ethereal. For an instant, I thought I could hear drums thrumming in the background, ominous and powerful, but it was just my own heart.

I would have made his hair into angel wings – something soft and that only the most worthy would be able to touch. I would be willing to paint his image across the baby grand if I had to, its slick, black surface bare in comparison to the man manipulating its keys. Unable to wait any longer, I walked up to the side of the piano bench, close enough to see his fingers pressing on the keys. His movements were awkward and jerky, as if he were hesitant about touching the next key, but I was only able to catch a glimpse. Once he became aware of my presence, his hands froze, and his head tilted up. My eyes met a set of blue, nearly clear, orbs. I opened my mouth to speak, but found no words befitting the situation. Why had I gone up there in the first place?

Thankfully, I didn't have to say anything. The spotlights dimmed, blanketing the entire room in darkness before the auditorium lights clicked on. They were yellow and ugly, but I was thankful for the momentary distraction. I studied the man again, finding his blue eyes still trained on me, but I found myself drawn more to the mischievous arch in his brow, and the one-sided smirk covering his lips.

While I had once deemed him an angel, the rest of him, paired with the depressing black ensemble, gave him qualities befitting a devil. My thrumming heart slowed with the realization, and I was disappointed to find his blue eyes were much less alluring when reflecting the yellowed lights. Whatever spell he had cast on me before, had disappeared, and I was instantly reminded of the reason I had come to the auditorium instead of the International Student Affairs Office.

I didn't hold back the frown that made its way to my lips, and my eyes drifted over to the backstage exit, where the head of International Student Affairs stood. He was a short man, not much taller than five foot, and his stomach protruded to the point where I often questioned how he was able to tie his shoes every morning. I assumed he slept in them. I had never cared for the man, not because he was rude or mean, but something about him always managed to rub me the wrong way. I was sure it would be no different now as he waddled his way toward us, clapping his hands and shifting his gaze back and forth between the two of us.

"Klemens, I have been waiting for you! I see you have already met Dominik Engel."

My gaze drifted to the man at the piano bench, but he was already back to studying the piano keys. He didn't dare press them, instead settling for brushing them with the tips of his fingers.

"Engel?" I said. "Are you German?"

The man stopped his ministrations and dropped his hands to his lap, then tilted his head back to peer at me again. He narrowed his gaze, then pouted his lips. It was an odd response, one that I hadn't expected. I looked to the head administrator for an answer, but even he was acting strange, shaking his head and giggling.

"Klemens, pardon me," he said apologetically. "I should have told you before. He doesn't speak English." He pressed a finger to his lips, and cast his gaze upward,

"Well, I guess that's not quite right. He understands a little, but he can't respond very well."

I still didn't get it. I understood introducing him to me, but that was just common courtesy. These details didn't mean a thing to me. I was going to just brush it off as another one of the head's odd ramblings when he stepped closer, pudgy hands wrapping around my arms.

"But that's why I need you, Klemens." He flashed his most needy expression, and continued on. "I know you're busy, but just wait until I tell you who this is."

I rolled my eyes and did my best to avoid the onslaught of onion breath, "Head, please excuse my rudeness, but did you not already tell me who this is?"

The head, thankfully, released his grip on me, but remained close enough that I could still smell the onions. He crossed his arms over his chest and snarled, "You know that's not what I mean." Then, his face relaxed into a proud smile, and he motioned toward Engel, "He is our newest musical art student, a vocalist, famous for his voice in Germany, and I personally recommended you as a perfect duet partner."

I froze. Me? Klemens Reinstadler, part of a duet? My musical lineage and ancestry be damned if I required a partner. The emotion must have been plastered across my face, because the head began to splutter comforting phrases, hands raised as if he were about to be hit.

"Now Klemens, there is no need to get upset. Hear me out. Take this as compliment." He was scrambling at this point, raking his hands through what little hair he had left. "You are a wonderful performer - one of the best. Plus, you can probably understand him better. Please? Give it some thought?"

I wanted to tell him that comparing Austrian and German is like comparing apples and oranges, but I held back. I didn't see how I was going to be able to help the German any more than the ISA office could, but if it would get the head out of my hair for a while, I'd be willing to try. I looked to the German again, and was surprised to find his lips moving, but with no sound as he brushed his hands along the keyboard. I would be lying if I said that he didn't make me curious. Just how great a singer was Engel? And did he have any other hidden musical talents?

I didn't get the chance to find out, as my phone chimed, signaling time for my next class. I had wasted the rest of my class, plus the rest of my break, and would probably have to sprint to make it to his next class on time. I would run. I hated to sweat, but I hated tardiness even more.

So, with a sigh, I responded, "Fine, fine. Is that all?"

I had already begun to turn when the head continued, "Dominik will be here every day after your classes. He has his own special tutor in our offices, so we'll send him here when it gets close."

I paused and asked, "If he has a tutor who can speak German, why do I have to watch him?"

The head frowned, "Klemens. The tutor has other students to look after. He can't just leave them alone for one student." Then he crossed his arms, a sign that the discussion was ending, "Besides, you've already agreed. Dominik will see you tomorrow." He looked to Engel and then motioned him over.

The German nodded, standing up and walking around the bench, but not without first brushing shoulders with me. I met his eyes, and he gave me a coy smile. I tried to smile back, but it felt too awkward for me to pull it off properly. I watched as the two men disappeared behind the backstage exit, but I didn't leave as quickly as I should have. Instead, I stuck around the piano, pressing the middle C and listening to it ring out in the empty auditorium. The key was still warm where Engel had pressed it. I blushed at the thought.

2 – THE FANFARE

I was punctual by default, and I had an issue with people who weren't quite as timely as I was. I stood outside the auditorium door, one hand poised on the handle, the other gripping my phone. It was two minutes before six. My last class had ended at five thirty, which had given me plenty of time to make it back to the music hall. Yesterday had been a whirlwind of new information, and I winced at the thought of having to relive more of it this evening. All I really wanted to do was go in, play a few pieces, unwind, then go home and prepare for it all again. Unfortunately, it wouldn't go that smoothly. I let out a deep sigh as another minute ticked by. It was time to go in.

I twisted the handle, slipped my phone back into my pocket, and stepped into the room. My eyes were trained directly on the stage, but there was no one there. No tinkling from the piano, no calm blue-hued spotlight, and no Dominik Engel. Was I surprised? Not nearly as much as I should have been. I scowled at the empty stage and shook my head, despite there being no one to witness it, and the chiming of my phone only frustrated me more. I pulled it out and switched off the alarm before sliding it right back in my pocket. I decided that if he wasn't coming, I would at least practice, and part of practice was preparing the mood.

Instead of heading toward the stage, I ducked into a door, well-hidden at the back of the auditorium. The only indication of it being there was the black handle, but even it blended into the black fabric along the walls. The studio was at the very top of the staircase, and inside was a console splattered with blinking, colorful buttons and dials. It had taken me at least two weeks to learn the basics, and I still wasn't sure about the more advanced controls, but I could light the room.

As I picked a dial and began to play around with the different types of spotlights, I was reminded of Dominik, sitting at the piano with nothing more than a single blue-tinted spotlight. He had looked angelic and ethereal, completely at ease with himself and the piano. It was beautiful. One of the most intimate scenes I had ever seen. I wanted that feeling while I played, and as I clicked through the different lights and hues, I never took my eyes off the piano. Eventually, I did find the blue hue, barely visible except for the reflection from the piano's surface. At the same time the spotlight clicked into place, my duet partner arrived, and he stepped onto the stage strolling directly to my piano.

He had a certain gait about him, an aura that bled confidence and pride. He stood by the bench, studying the keys with great intensity, and seemingly unaware that I was not in the room. I studied him just as much as he studied the keys, noticing the blue seeping into the thin ends of his hair and the way his skin softened beneath the light. He was truly a sight to behold, and I found myself in awe as I drank in his silhouette. All of those thoughts heated my cheeks, and my heart thrummed in my chest as his eyes shifted from the piano and directly up to the control box.

At first he didn't react, and I wondered if he could even see me through the spotlight, but then he smiled, a crooked smile, which didn't quite match his angelic image. I waved to him, though the movement was much more of an awkward flail than anything else. Dominik either didn't notice or was too polite to laugh, and instead motioned toward the auditorium lights, which still leaked their orange-yellow hue, save for where the spotlight centered onto the stage. I nodded in return and flipped the main switch, which dimmed the lights, leaving the blue spotlight as the only source beaming on the stage. I looked to Dominik again and he shot me a thumbs up before motioning me to come down.

It struck me as odd how everything seemed so familiar to him, as if he had been doing it for years. But I didn't remain too long in thought as I realized the lights in the control box and stairway had also dimmed, except for the buttons, which blinked at me mockingly. I turned to the staircase and fumbled my way down the steps, trying to take my time, but also fighting with my need to be on time and practice. I made it down without too much trouble and worked my way up to the stage where Dominik had already set up his microphone stand. He met my gaze and nodded in approval, then went back to his own preparations. I didn't spare a second glance, instead focusing solely on the piece of music laid against the piano stand.

I took a seat first, being careful to not disturb the bench from its perfect positioning. Then I plucked the single page of music from the stand, surprised at first by its length, or lack thereof. But when I read the title, I had to readjust my glasses a few times just to be sure I was reading it correctly.

"Die Lorelei?" I looked to Dominik, his back toward me as I sent him an appalled scowl, "We're playing German folk songs now?"

There was nothing wrong with a German folk song, but I was annoyed that he would only pick a song from his home country, especially when mine had such a large variety of classical tunes from which to pick. But no, he settled for a folk song, one his mother might have played him at Christmas when he was a young boy. It had bile rising in my throat. But Dominik didn't say a word. Instead he turned around to shoot me a glare sharp enough to physically cut someone. I swallowed back any more retorts, and waited patiently for him to turn back again, but he took much longer than I would've liked. He continued to stare, unnerving me, and just to avoid looking at him any longer, I busied myself with putting the music back on the stand.

Finally, he said, "Play." His German accent was thick, much thicker than I would've expected from any transfer student, even one who had little to no knowledge of the English language.

It was jarring to hear, but I tried to brush it off, just thankful that he had refocused on practice. I steadied my hands on the keys, took a deep breath, and began to play. I started somber and slow, much slower than the piece called for, but it fit well with the melody. My sad melody only lasted for so long, a few bars, and I had to break, leaving the air empty and open for the singer to cut in. There was a slight pause, only a few seconds, which allowed the final note to dance a bit before Dominik came in. Then, I listened.

He took his time beginning, allowing the first note to drag and ache. He sounded just as pained as my piano had, and it had my chest clenching. My fingers quivered as I came back in, much softer than I had originally, but gradually crescendoed to match Dominik as his voice rose.

The song was about a captain of a ship, lured by a sea-maiden. He was enchanted by her voice and beauty. She was a siren, and not unlike Dominik in both talent and looks. The captain ultimately met his death at sea, but he regretted nothing. Hearing her voice was worth the loss.

Dominik's voice lilted, and the hue I once thought to be angelic became something more. It was something painful, not unlike losing a lover or the death of a close friend. My eyes were growing misty and it took every ounce of concentration I had to continue to read the page.

His deep pain eventually faded into a deep bitterness, which fell off him in waves, but even that faded away to deep hums. The piano hummed back, and our sounds intertwined and became a single voice. We shared the stage. Then, Dominik's voice returned and he sang the final verse as I petered off into a much softer, dwindling version of the melody. His voice rose far above that of my piano, and I could almost imagine that his eyes shut tight as he belted out the final notes to what should have been a full audience. At the very end his voice cracked, fading back to reveal the sound of my piano, still petering in the background until the final note sounded. But the final note didn't end, it trailed on, and far past my piano, and I ripped my gaze away from the music long enough to peer at Dominik. He was turning around to face me, his clear eyes meeting mine and revealing a deep emptiness and longing.

My heart was thrumming in my ears, deafening the echoes of his voice and leaving the original sound for my ears alone. And just as his mouth closed over the final note, my phone chimed to life with Ode to Joy. I tugged it out of my pocket. My brother. I wasn't surprised. I looked back to Dominik, but he was already undoing the microphone stand and preparing to leave. I let out a sigh, and accepted my brother's call.

I bit back the growl in my voice and did my best to speak calmly, "Hallo, Bernard."

After our first practice together, which had been much shorter than I had planned, Dominik and I were practicing every day at the same time. We played classics spanning all countries and time periods, and I was no less enthralled by his voice than I had been the first time. But there was always something missing. Dominik's voice was beautiful and rang in my ears long after we had finished practicing, but none as much as the German folk song. He executed all others wonderfully, but they lacked the emotion and devotion he had carried in Die Lorelei.

But one evening, no more than a week after our first practice, I noted a staleness in the air. Every song had finished much shorter and stunted than had been the case only a few days prior. It was disconcerting and had me reviewing the past practices in great detail. We had performed plenty of pieces, which had been in many different languages and signatures, but Dominik had never spoken. He always brought in a folder with all the music he wanted to perform, and he would set it on the stand every day before I even got to the auditorium. As I set up the music for myself, he would prepare the microphone. It was a routine we picked up immediately, but it left me wondering. Why did he never speak? It wasn't as if he spoke no English at all. We had performed plenty of English songs, which he sang with perfect enunciation and clarity.

I was interested in his normal voice. What did it sound like? I had only heard him say one word and that wasn't enough to reveal anything about him. As Dominik took his microphone off the stand and prepared to leave for the day, my thoughts drifted back to that one word. His accent had been thick, much thicker than the average German accent, and I knew it. Being in the ISA Office for so long, I had been around plenty of other students from Germany and other corners of the world, and I never heard an accent as thick as his.

"Dominik," I narrowed my eyes in his direction and he turned to look at me. "Why don't you ever speak?"

He stared, at me blankly, as if he were trying to come up with an answer. Then the corners of his lips turned up into a smile, but he didn't speak.

I tried again, "I think you're holding back. I want to know why."

Dominik chuckled, running a hand through his feathery blond hair, then responded, "No one has ever asked me." He shrugged, "Why speak when no one cares to listen?"

His words made sense to me, but I couldn't quite wrap my head around the fact that he had been able to speak and still chose not to. I was never one to be extremely talkative or vocal, but I couldn't imagine resigning myself into complete silence. That was a concept beyond my understanding, but Dominik's smile was infectious, and I couldn't help smiling back before continuing.

"I suppose you're right, but," and I shifted my gaze back to my lap before I continued, "I just can't imagine pretending to be mute. How did you manage such a thing?"

Dominik remained silent for a while, except for the constant sound of him wrapping the cord of the microphone around and around his hand. I cut a sideways glace and caught him frowning at the wire, as if it were a problem needing to be solved. It was the most serious I had seen him since he had first played on the piano. Once he found whatever he was searching for, he looked up, and I quickly shifted my gaze back my lap.

"Well, let me put it this way. It's much easier to make it through life when people don't expect much from you." I looked at him again, but was surprised to find him smiling, despite the depressing tone of his words. "Besides, it gives me the chance to surprise people. Right, Klem?"

I scowled at the use of the nickname, but had to smile at the surprise. He was right. I never would've guessed that he could speak clear English had it not been for his performances in English. But I wondered about what else he hid from the world, what other mysteries there were beneath his angelic exterior. Though his eyes were nearly-clear colored when he performed, they were blue shields now as we spoke. It was strange how vulnerable he could be one second, then guarded the next.

I was so lost in thought that I hadn't noticed the German scrutinizing me. At least, not until he spoke. "On the phone after our first practice, you said an Austrian name. Is that a friend? Family? Lover?" and his eyes froze me in place at that last guess, while his lips curled into a mischievous smirk.

The question itself wasn't what made me blush, but the emphasis he had placed, paired with his false, thick German accent, made it all seem more personal and revealing. I wasn't sure how to answer at first, and it took me a moment to realize it hadn't been a lover at all. I was still embarrassed to speak. Dominik's gaze never wavered, but I did eventually manage to get something out.

"Not that it is your business, but it was my brother."

The German didn't smirk anymore, but lapsed into a soft smile. He looked comfortable and pleased with my answer, but for what reason I couldn't be sure, and that made me all the more uncomfortable. Silence blanketed the auditorium, but the awkward feeling was potent. I tried my best to distract myself by pecking at the piano keys, but it only managed to heighten my anxiety. Instead, I attempted conversation.

"Dominik, do you have siblings?"

For once, I seemed to stump Dominik. His usual casual demeanor broke into a confused, blank stare, and I would be lying if I didn't say I was a bit proud of that fact. I tried my best to remain neutral, and I was doing a fine job of it until his stare morphed into a shield of ice and his mouth fell into a deep set frown. Wrinkles I didn't know could exist on such a young man were carving themselves into the corners of his mouth, and it took every ounce of self-control I had to not reach up and attempt to smooth them out. I regretted having asked the question. I expected no answer and was about to apologize for prying when he finally responded.

"I have a brother. We're army brats."

The final sentence shocked me, and my eyebrows shot up in response, but I pursed my lips and went back to cleaning up the stage. While I was interested, and I couldn't imagine Dominik having anything to do with war, I refrained from prying any further. I didn't want him to shy away from me any further than he already had. We remained silent for the rest of the evening, cleaning in our own separate parts of the stage before departing for our dorms.

We didn't say a word to each other, but that didn't stop my mind from wandering. I questioned every imaginary fact I could conjure, and ended up with an image of Dominik that kept me blushing even after I had made it to my dorm and into bed. Did Dominik play the piano? I wasn't sure, but the thought kept me up that night, along with an image of us sitting at the piano as I led his hands back and forth across the keys.

3 – THE FIRST STRAIN

The next day couldn't have gone by any more slowly. I was tired, not because I hadn't slept, but because of the drag of the day. I was a timely student. A punctual student. I was never the teachers' pet, but when the teachers took notice of my scores and abilities, they would often praise me. I tried not to make it too big of a deal, but it happened, regardless. As I sat in class, I found myself drifting. My pen rested lifelessly on a blank page, while my eyes surveyed the room. I purposefully avoided my teacher as he went on with whatever lesson he had planned. Was it history or math? I couldn't recall.

I had drifted from class to class, a shadow amongst the lighted halls. All the while, I thought of the practice which awaited me, the German sitting at the piano, his fingers dancing across the keys. I physically shook myself and trained my eyes on the teacher. I tried to piece together the snippets of the lecture I would catch. My pen never moved, but my eyes eventually began to shift again from student to student. They all looked indifferent, some writing, some not, but they all had their minds elsewhere.

My heart lurched in my chest, and I found myself

wondering if I had been the only one to ever diligently take notes and study. My heart and mind had always been in my studies and my music. For the first time since I had started the University, I wondered about my colleagues. I wasn't always a complete recluse, but those moments were rare and only when the teacher demanded we work in groups. The rest of the time, it might as well have been just the teacher and me. Depending on the class, it might as well have just been me. But seeing those empty faces with their glazed eyes had me curious. What did they think of while they avoided their studies?

Was it other courses? Maybe. Were there parties? Clubs? Friends? The weekend? Did they think of small, insignificant things, like what they would have for lunch or dinner? Or were their thoughts filled with things like jobs, money and love? It haunted me to realize that I had never thought of such things. My life had always consisted of the same, punctual schedule. Why had I never stopped to think about things like what I would have for lunch? I would've thought more on the subject had the lecture continued.

Unfortunately, I drifted back into reality long enough to catch the tail end of my professor releasing us for the evening. It took me a while to comprehend everyone moving about and stuffing books back into packed bags, while they discussed things that they had probably been thinking about for the entire class period. It made the weight of my heart lift and left me hollow. No one turned to look at me. No one stopped to ask what I was having for lunch or dinner. Nobody even looked my way. Did Dominik feel just as lonely as I did, even in a room full of people?

The thought was even more powerful when my eyes fell back to the blank sheet of paper on my desk. I didn't even have anyone to ask for notes. I had never needed help before, nor did I ever need another person – for companionship or otherwise. Sitting in the classroom as everyone, including the teacher, left to go on with their lives, I found myself even more alone than I had ever felt in my entire life. I ground my pen into the paper, leaving a jagged line across the top of the page. It was a relief to see it come across and eliminate the emptiness, but there just wasn't enough to fill the lines. I sat silently staring at the line for what felt like ages. I eventually got up and began to pack my own bag, but it was only after shifting into autopilot.

I tried to remain blank as I slung the backpack over my shoulder and picked up my violin case, cradling it against my chest. But once I entered the hallway to find the other students filtering into other rooms or heading back to the dorms, I was met once more with silence. I dipped my head and thought of Dominik, sitting quietly at the back of a classroom where no one knew he spoke English, nor did they care. Was this how he felt walking down the hallways? Was he a shadow amongst the lighted halls?

I stood outside the concert hall well past the time I usually would. I hated being late, even more so than I hated anything else. It just felt wrong to not be at the right place at the right time. It ruined the flow. But today wasn't flowing as it should have, and it continued even as I stared at the door of the auditorium. It had never occurred to me to just open the door and go inside, even after I heard the chiming of my alarm. I didn't even take the time to turn it off. I just stood there and let the sound bounce around the empty hallways. It felt fuller that way and much better than the empty silence, but even it faded away. I was left once again with only my thoughts as company.

Dominik was inside. He had to be. Either that, or he was late, just like me. For a second, I found a smile tugging at the corners of my lips. The thought of me being late with Dominik made me smile, but then I thought about him at the piano, and drifted back into the imaginary auditorium inside my mind. He was pecking at the keys, just as he had the first day I met him, but he wasn't alone. I stood at the front of the stage, toes just barely skirting the edge. I held my violin. I hadn't played my violin on a stage in years.

I turned to look at Dominik, expecting his eyes to be focused solely on the piano, but I found his gaze trained on me. His lips curved up into a smirk, and his blue eyes danced beneath the shimmering blue light. The blond locks, which usually fell across his forehead and the sides of his face seemed to lift and sway from a non-existent breeze. His hair billowed up and faded out to look like angel wings. How was it possible he could have a mischievous smile, but an angelic form? I supposed I would never know.

The imaginary me smiled back, a genuine and carefree smile, one I hadn't shown in a long time. I don't think I ever smiled like that. It was strange seeing myself from the outside, but I had to remind myself that it was imaginary. As much as I wanted it to be real, everything I was seeing was of my own creation, and all in my head. Such a thought didn't dampen the image at all.

Either way, the imaginary me turned back to face the empty seats of the auditorium, black and blurred in the darkness. I didn't seem to mind and bowed as I would had there been people there. I heard a faint, short laugh from behind me, but the tinkling of the piano drowned out its existence. The imaginary me shook my head, as if to clear my mind before resting the violin against the top of my shoulder, then I placed my chin in the rest before settling the bow against the taut strings.

Like I said before, I wasn't one to choose the violin over my piano. Something about the piano felt safe and kept me hidden and comfortable, but the violin in that instance felt right. The openness of it all had made me feel free and vulnerable to the world - something I wasn't in my real life. And as I opened the private concert with a gradual ritardando, the fear of failure and openness fell away. I was no longer alone, and the tinkling of the piano behind me only managed to punctuate that point. I made my entrance grand, like the Austrian I held deep inside of myself.

Then the imaginary me did something I would never have dared to do in real life, especially during a concert. I turned back toward Dominik, continuing to scrape the bow across the strings, and watched as Dominik's hands bounced across the keys. It was a form no professional would ever allow, but it was perfect for him. He made it seem graceful and artistic, though a pianist would say he was clumsy and without purpose or form. The thought made me laugh. The scene was a rich mixture of imperfect perfection, and it made my heart swell with pure unkempt emotion. It made my eyes water.

But the imaginary world would only hold up for so long. Dominik's eyes lit on mine and his mouth opened as if to sing, but what came out was simply his voice, much louder than I would've expected with so much sound echoing around the auditorium.

"What are you doing?"

A simple question, but one powerful enough to pull me straight out of my imaginary auditorium back to the empty hallway. Empty except for me and Dominik, who stared at me with a look of both curiosity and concern. My face was burning and my lungs felt heavy as they pumped the huge gulps of air I struggled to get down. My vision was cloudy, and I was embarrassed to find that I was pressed flush against the door, hand gripping the heated door knob with force enough to crush another man's hand.

"Feeling all right Klem?"

I loathed the nickname, but I was too ill to say anything. Instead, I focused on calming my heaving chest.

All the while Dominik stared at me. It didn't make me uncomfortable, but I turned my face away from him just to retain some privacy. We remained like that for what seemed like eternity until Dominik spoke again.

"What were you doing?"

I looked his way again, unsurprised by the devilish smirk on his face. He wanted to say something. I was sure of it, but there was no way I could handle him being foolish. Pushing myself upright, I resettled my clothing, then went back to opening the door.

"Can we talk about this later? We've wasted enough time just standing around."

But Dominik was having none of it. He pushed his way in front of the door and shoved my hand back against my chest. He was extremely close, close enough that I could smell cinnamon on his breath when he laughed. What had he eaten that would have cinnamon in it? Regardless, the smell was hot and made me crinkle my nose. Even worse was the proximity of our bodies. He left his hand on my wrist, even after he had pressed it to my chest, and our knees continued to knock into each other even after I had shuffled backward. Dominik didn't seem to care, his face still playful and inviting. He was waiting for something, and he wasn't going to move until he got it.

It was then I was struck with the strangest and most inappropriate thought I had had in a long time. Maybe he wanted me to kiss him. The image crossed my mind and seemed to imprint there. No matter how many times I tried to rethink it, I ended up making it worse. Would he taste like cinnamon? Would his lips feel as feathery soft as his hair looked? Did he want to kiss me?

My face was heating up again and as I looked up to meet Dominik's eyes, only to find that he had noticed. His smile fell away to a frown, and his hand released my wrist so he could take my shoulders in both of his hands. Every time I had seen him play the piano, his hands had looked dainty and fragile. While they were still beautiful, they were much bigger than I had expected. Dominik was a big man in general, but lean. I was lean and of average height, though I had been called short on more than one occasion. And while I focused on him, he was studying me.

"Are you feeling ok? Is something wrong?"

I opened my mouth to respond, but nothing was coming to me. I was unable to form a single word. I was too focused on his hands on my shoulders and his knees bumping into mine. There was too much going on, too much for my brain to process, and I had given up trying to respond before I realized he was rubbing my shoulders. Something about that simple movement, though comforting, changed me. I went from flustered to frightened within seconds, and I wasn't one for abrupt mood changes, much less outbursts.

But as soon as I felt those hands, heavy and calloused, massaging my shoulders, I fumbled backward, shaking my head furiously as I nearly yelled, "No! No! I'm fine!"

Dominik froze, his hands still out-reaching. I took in a lungful of air, trying to calm my racing heart and to cool my heated face, but it was for naught. Dominik was at a loss, and when he dropped his arms to his sides, clenching and un-clenching his hands, I knew he truly had no idea what to do. In all honesty, I didn't either. It was awkward, and I had the social grace of a water buffalo. Dominik on the other hand seemed suave and prepared for situations like that, but as I watched him fidget and avoid my gaze, I realized that he was just as uncomfortable as I was. The thought of him at the back of a classroom, alone and restless came to the forefront of my mind and all I wanted to do was take him into my arms.

Instead, I tried to play it off and began brushing down the front of my shirt, "I'm fine. Now, can we please get practice started?"

I paused and met Dominik's gaze. He remained silent and in deep thought, but his eyes were constantly moving.

They roved up and down my face, glazed and without purpose. He was somewhere else, and he reminded me of all the people I sat with in class. I had never felt so alone in his presence. In the end, he didn't say another word. He simply nodded, turned away from me and slipped into the concert hall - out of my sight and allowing me a little time to mourn my own loneliness. It was a pitiful feeling and I'm sure it was an even more pitiful sight. I was just thankful I had been given the chance to let it out alone, though the empty hall was the reason it had occurred in the first place. Regardless, I sucked it up.

I did one final sweep across the front of my shirt, straightening out the non-existent wrinkles, then took in a deep breath before opening the door and sweeping into the auditorium. My entrance was loud and echoed off the architecture of the room, but I did not flinch. I held my head high and stomped up to the stage, all the while Dominik pretended to be unaware of my presence. It made my stomach ache, but I continued my march without showing anything. I didn't know if he cared or not, but I cared, and that's all I wanted to show.

I made it up to the stage and took my place beside the piano where a small packet of music was tucked neatly behind the piano stand. Dropping my bags at the side of the piano, I pulled it out and sat at the bench while I tried to focus solely on flipping through the pieces. Die Lorelei was the only piece to catch my eye, but I did my best to avoid it. At least twenty pieces of music, surely there was something else I felt like playing. After a few minutes of useless flipping, I eventually settled on the German folk song, though not without a frustrated sigh. I set the piece on the stand, then placed my fingers on the keys to start the tune.

I sat like that in silence for a good while, waiting for Dominik to start us off. I hadn't noticed the silence until then. I looked toward the front of the stage, surprised to find him standing there, completely still and looking at me.

It was a shock at first and I immediately began to panic as my self-consciousness began to take hold. But then I studied him. He held the microphone in his left hand as if it were a scepter, while unconsciously gripping the stand in his other. The light shone down on him in a way that cast shadow across the front of his features, hiding all but the glowing outline of his silhouette and his crystalline blue gaze. He reminded me of a king, and I dare to say he even resembled an archangel.

In that instance, I found my hands running cold and they felt awkward pressed against the keys. I wanted to play my violin. My eyes drifted over to my bag, propped up against the leg of the piano, but my violin bag was impossible to make out. The itch was maddening, and when my eyes met Dominik's again, I knew that he should have been sitting at the piano instead. But he only smiled at me and shook his head before mumbling, "The folk song?"

I'm not sure why, but I smiled back. I guess I could say that his smile was contagious, but that wouldn't be the truth. His smile heated my cheeks and my chest. My heart fluttered from the heat and purred just beneath my sternum. It was a strange feeling, to say the least. I nodded in response, savoring the silence and perfection of the moment. His smile never faltered, even as he held the microphone up to his mouth and whispered a count off, and he never turned back toward the empty auditorium.

His eyes remained locked with mine as he began to sing, and my fingers moved without much thought. I could've played the song in my sleep, and the piece of music sat on the stand abandoned while I watched Dominik. His stride was slow at first and managed to get slower and slower the closer he got to the piano. It was frustrating, and by the time he made it to the piano the song had almost ended. He planned it that way, I'm sure. I expected him to just stand there until the song finished. Instead, he switched off the microphone, though his voice seemed just as loud and clear without it, then slid onto the stool beside me. It took everything I had not to fumble as our elbows brushed and his gaze shifted to my hands.

It was intimate. His voice rang in my ears, his gaze heated my hands, and his body so close to mine as I played had me dizzy. It was the best performance of my entire life, and there wasn't even an audience to enjoy it. It didn't matter. It was better that it was just us - as if the performance were for us and us alone. Something about having Dominik so close and it only being us had me nervous, much more nervous than I had ever been with a packed house. I kept having to remind myself: I could play that song any day, at anytime, anywhere and on any instrument, but no amount of reassurance could contain my need for absolute perfection. I wanted to show my very best, even if Dominik was the only one to ever see it.

I finished the tune and Dominik tapered off along with it, leaving the room to echo the memory of our special performance - a concert for two. Dominik's eyes left my poised hands, shifting up my arms, to my neck, all the way up to my eyes, leaving a trail of heat in its wake. With my whole body warm, my chest started to heave and my lungs were having a harder and harder time pushing out any air. I wondered what Dominik thought of me, what he thought of our performance, if he was as enamored and out of breath as I was, but he just looked at me. He wasn't breathing any differently than he had before, and his blue eyes were as clear as gems. Then his petal pink lips parted and my breath caught in my throat as he asked, "Can you teach me?"

I'm not sure how long it took me to register his words. I sat mute for at least ten minutes, studying his face, but not really seeing him. I just sat and soaked in his words. What had I expected? What had I been waiting for him to say to me? He hadn't rushed me. Instead, he had let me sit and focus solely on my hands, still pressed and arched against the keys - ready to play at a moment's notice. He placed his hands alongside mine, trying to mimic every muscle and arch in my fingers. His form was still that of an amateur, and his pinkies dangled lost at the ends of his hands while he focused too hard on getting the other fingers to match. I choked back a laugh and shook my head.

"You're forgetting the pinky."

His eyes trailed back to my face, but I failed to catch the expression.

"Can you?"

"Can I what?"

He pressed the keys, the sound tinkling from the piano in a series of mismatched chords. He waited until the sound died away before he asked again, "Can you teach me?"

I didn't speak again for a long time, the sounds of the piano still echoing in my mind. My eyes fell to his hands again, so close to mine that I could feel the heat and intensity radiating from the very tips of his fingers. A smile tugged at the corners of my mouth, but it didn't quite make it to my face.

"Of course. Do you want to start now?"

4 – THE SECOND STRAIN

Practice from then on out was much different than what I had come to expect. It was light-hearted, peaceful, and, dare I say, fun. Dominik and I no longer focused on specific pieces and our separate parts, we focused on learning, laughing and enjoying the music - whether it was well-executed or not, did not matter. It was something I had never experienced. It was something that I wished would last forever. I would pick a random piece, teach Dominik the notes, and allow him to peck around on the piano at his own pace. I didn't correct him as often as I probably should have, and I didn't take the time to correct the posture of his hands. It would've ruined it, I think. Those moments would have been too sterile, and I think he felt the same.

He was confident with every piece I put before him. He never questioned me over a note or a rhythm. He played what I taught him the best he could, and that was enough for the both of us. Though the practice in itself was wonderful, what made it truly special was the conversation. When Dominik tired of a piece, and I point out that Dominik would tire of it because I never tired of watching his hands move across the keys, he would stop playing and promptly rest his hands in his lap, then dive right into conversation. We talked about our lives, about what we would be doing in our classes, how we felt about one thing or another. It was the most personal I had ever become with another human being, and it happened so often that I couldn't imagine my life without it after that. How had I existed so long without such simple human interaction?

It was another of our wonderful practices, and we had just completed a Sonata - the bare bones to a march. It was simple and didn't require much skill to perform, but it had always been one of my favorites. It had been slow going for Dominik to learn, and he was uncharacteristically focused on learning, leaving little time for our fireside chats. Regardless, I had enjoyed watching him progress until he could play the Sonata with as much ease as a professional. But after his fifth successful play-through, I was ready to call it a night. After collecting all the music we had strewn about the stage, I was done. Something about our practices made me careless, something I wasn't capable of during the day. It was both a pleasure and a pain as I was the one who had to clean up afterward.

The cleaning was stressful and tended to press upon my bitter side. In those moments, I wanted nothing more than to fade back and recall who I truly was. I went back and remembered small moments in time, moments which defined the very essence of my being. The moment I picked up the violin for the first time, the last time I had played my violin, the day I had confessed to my first girlfriend, and the day I ended my relationship with my first girlfriend. The list went on and on. But even as I listed it all, something seemed off. I paused and rethought my list. Each time I went over it, I stumbled over my relationship.

I had only ever had one relationship in my past, and it was with a woman, a Hungarian woman, much to my mother's dismay. It was probably the most rebellious I had been in my entire life. I had thought she was beautiful, but I never lusted after her. We were platonic and our relationship tapered out soon after it had begun. My mother was pleased. We had retained our friendship, but even that had begun to disappear once I left for America. Other than that short stint, I had been single. No. Not single. I had been alone.

Once I had gone through my list and past, I found myself panicking. I had no reason to panic, but some detail I had overlooked was weighing heavily on me. What was I not seeing? What had I been blind to all this time? With no answer, I plunged deeper into my anxiety. My breath quickened as did my heart, while my lungs struggled to keep up the pace. I had no time to think, no time to concentrate, and Dominik's voice was lost on my deaf ears as he attempted to hold some conversation with me. Had my heart always beaten so loud? It didn't matter. I couldn't force myself to look at him and instead tried to direct all of my focus and energy on organizing the music by composer last name. Haydn with Haydn, Mozart with Mozart - clarity, order, and common sense. I was already feeling better, but I still couldn't bring myself to look at Dominik. It was still too soon, but I had to respond to him. I couldn't imagine what he was thinking, and just thinking of what he was thinking had my mind reeling. I just had to focus on his words, just on his words.

"What was that, Dominik?"

Dominik didn't hesitate or question why I hadn't responded the first time he spoke, which comforted me just a bit. Dominik asked, "Why did you decide to become a musician?"

It was a topic I loved, and one which required little thought on my part. Plus, it was a blessing - a distraction from the turmoil, which raged just beneath the surface. My breathing settled as my thoughts trailed down to the hobby of my affections, and the sweat which had begun to bead on my forehead cooled and seemed to just freeze upon my skin. I attempted to wipe it dry against the back of my hand. The small movement felt natural and the warmth of my hand against my forehead eased me even more. In my state of content, I took the chance to clear my throat and my thoughts. I dropped my hand to my side and met Dominik's even gaze with a firm gaze of my own.

"Well, my mother played piano and my father the violin." Once all of the music had been neatly stacked and put down, I strode back to the piano where I could give it a loving caress, then I continued, "My grandmother played the clarinet. My grandfather sang in the opera."

As I continued to list family member after family member, my skin tingled with excitement. I couldn't be more proud of my Austrian roots. The very blood which rushed through my veins thrummed with the talent and power of every musician from every branch of our Austrian family. It made me who I was, just as much as music made me who I was. While I spilled every name and instrument in my family tree, Dominik sat stiff and silent. I hadn't even noticed until after I had finished my list, and even then I was so caught up in the air of my own pride that I failed to notice Dominik's uneasy look.

"So, you do it because it's a family thing?"

Caught off guard, I shot him a glare. His tone rang out as dismissive, a tone which offended the prideful Austrian within me and seemed to lock up my muscles. I did my best to loosen up and calm my face, but it didn't feel successful.

"Of course not! Why would you say such a thing?"

He shrugged. His lack of enthusiasm only managed to burn me more. "I don't know. All I hear are names and instruments. None of them have anything to do with you."

I blanched, "Nothing to do with me? Their blood

runs through my veins. They couldn't be more connected to me if they tried!" I even pulled back the cuffs of my jacket, as if he could see their names inked across my skin in a pattern of blue veins.

He didn't seem interested. The panic was rising back up, and this time I had no other choice but to engage it head on. The only retort I could manage was in the form of a question, "Well fine, then why do you sing?"

I immediately regretted it. As soon as the words had left my mouth, Dominik seemed to curl into himself. His shoulders fell just as his face did, and his clear gaze grew colder like ice. He looked as if someone had just beaten him, and my hands burned as if I had been the one to hold the club. I wanted to take it back, but it was too late. My words hung in the air for what seemed like an eternity. They were thick and made my hands sticky, but it could've just been from the nervous sweat. I was so tired of sweating.

Eventually Dominik did pick up the slack, but his response didn't comfort me in the slightest.

"Because it makes me happy."

It was simple. It was concise. It was something my brain couldn't comprehend. My panic froze, my hands froze, my thoughts seemed to flow at the rate of ticker-tape. He only did it because it made him happy. What was the point in that? What goal was happiness? What was the purpose of happiness? It had never occurred to me that one could do something just because it made him happy. Every time I had ever sat down at the piano, I had a goal in mind. I was going to play whatever piece with the proficiency of a master. I wanted to play so I could capture the audience. I wanted the world to hear my sound and have them all freeze in awe. I wanted to play because it made my parents applaud me. I was left speechless. My thoughts had emptied until they were simple shells. Still, I tried to carry on.

"Don't your parents sing?" I winced as my voice

echoed around the auditorium. It was so flat, not even the architecture could give it a hint of texture.

Either Dominik didn't notice or didn't care as he continued on the topic, "Not at all." He shifted his gaze back to the piano before he continued, "My dad is a general, my mother- a proud army wife, and my brother," the next words came out of his mouth like an audible scowl, "is joining the army as soon as he graduates high school."

A military family. It all made sense. He came from a family of manly men. Men who fought wars, who married women to raise sons, who would then continue the tradition and join the war right along with their fathers. To lose a son to something like music or the arts in general would be considered a disgrace. It would've been the equivalent of me joining the army while my entire family was a part of the arts. My mother would drown in her own tears before she would allow such a thing, and my father would drown me in my mother's tears. Even the thought of disappointing them made me sick, and that weakness only managed to make me hate myself more.

All the while, the wheels in Dominik's head turned and turned. His stiff and dismissive features began to morph into something playful and hopeful. He looked like a small child, eyes as wide as saucers. I didn't think it was possible to have such an expressive face, but somehow Dominik always found a way to change his entire look. How many faces could one person have? How many different people did Dominik have inside him? I wanted to know so much more about Dominik, but such things would have to wait.

He smiled, a small and timid smile, as he asked, "What does your brother do?"

The question stumped me. It had nothing to do with any of the preceding conversation, and at any other time I would've brushed it off. But the way he looked at me, glassy orbs and clearing eyes, I had to. It seemed far too important to just leave unanswered. I sighed and ran a hand across my scalp.

"He's young." I sighed again, though it came out as more of a growl, "He's so young." I couldn't seem to stand still, fidgeting and playing with my hands. I tried to cross my arms, but I even managed to make that fidgety.

"He wants to be a painter. Mother started him on the clarinet, but," I paused long enough to shake my head, "he dropped it for a paint brush. She was mortified, but there's no denying he's talented at it."

Once I finished, I met Dominik's eyes and found his saucers had shrunk into slits, a glare. My body went stiff. My heart thrummed in rebellion, and I had to will myself not to go into panic mode. I was really getting sick of my own reactions, but there was little I could do to stop it. Dominik had a power over me. Even today I find it hard to explain. I wanted to say something to him, anything to shift the mood. I opened my mouth, then closed it again. I was at a loss for words, but Dominik had plenty of his own.

"Have you ever seen one of his paintings?"

I wasn't sure where he was headed, and I shook my head in response. I didn't trust my own words anymore.

He took in a deep breath and closed his eyes, "You haven't seen his paintings. You say he is young like it's a bad thing. How do you think that makes him feel?"

When he opened his eyes again, the usual clear blue was a much harder and cold blue. It made his presence so much more concrete than what I was used to seeing. He was so much more human to me. Sweat began to form across my brow, chilling the skin beneath as it rolled down my face. I really should have brought a kerchief. I tried to respond again, and I was successful in getting a few words out, but they weren't the ones I wanted.

"I wouldn't know."

Dominik's eyes widened, then he shut them as he shook his head and scrubbed his face with the palm of his hand. He paused in his scrubbing long enough to take a deep breath before lowering his hand. He didn't meet my eyes again.

"Have you at least seen his paintings?"

I paused to mull it over. Had I seen any of his paintings? I had seen him painting plenty of times, but I couldn't recall a time I had ever seen a single finished piece. He had a painting in a museum, how could I have missed that? It all left a sour feeling in my stomach. All I could do was shake my head in response. Dominik wasn't looking at me to see it, but by the way he sighed, I figured my silence was enough to answer his question.

Dominik didn't speak again. He jerked up out of his seat, the abruptness surprising me and causing me to jump. I tried to ask him where he was going, but my tongue might has well have been a slug for all the good it did me. All I could do was grumble as Dominik marched to the backstage exit. I watched him the entire way, but he never looked back, not until he was already standing halfway in the doorway. He turned back and looked at me, a sad smile molded over his mouth.

"Next time you hear from him, try telling him how proud you are. It'll make him very happy."

And with that, he turned back away and disappeared into the hallway. Left with silence and my own thoughts, the pressure of our conversation weighed heavily on me. For whatever reason, Dominik had made it much more personal than was necessary. He sounded invested in the situation between my brother and me. I wasn't sure how to react to it all, but it didn't matter if I was ready or not. As if right on cue, my phone began to chime. I pulled it from my pocket and answered without looking at the screen.

"Bernard?"

My voice cracked at the end of his name and the tears which poured down my cheeks left heated trails. I think I stayed in that music hall talking to him for at least three hours. It was the longest conversation I had ever had with my brother. He had painted me playing my violin once, but I couldn't recall ever seeing it.

5 – THE DOG FIGHT

The days slowed to a crawl after our disagreement. There was little I could say or do that didn't feel forced or awkward anymore. The days of comfort and casual banter were no more. Dominik didn't seem to mind. He continued to practice and practice, and he was learning the piano much faster than I could have imagined. One would've thought he was preparing for something. I tried to pretend that was the reason for our ever growing distance, but I could not lie to myself. At the time, I did not think our situation could get much worse, but it was only the beginning.

4:59 pm.

Right on time. While the rest of my world felt like it was falling apart, these little achievements made it all bearable. It felt like there was still hope, that time hadn't moved on and that I could go back. But as I entered the music hall, my eyes locked onto Dominik. His face was stern. He sat at the piano, hunched over, but not touching a single key. Something about his expression was hard, weathered. He was so much older than I remembered. It all brought me back to reality, and I was once again pressed with grief.

Though I was upset, something about him sitting there didn't feel right. He never came early for practice. It was something I had grown used to. This change, no matter how minute, had me sweating. Why hadn't I brought my kerchief? I tried to relax, smoothing my shirt out and running a hand through my hair, but all it did was reignite my self-consciousness. I didn't trust myself with my own feelings anymore. Instead, I slunk up to the stage and to the piano stool. I wasn't in the mood to deal with arguments or fake moments of friendship, but Dominik didn't scoot over.

I tried clearing my throat, but even that failed to get his attention. I stood there for at least five minutes, squirming, clearing my throat, and squirming some more. I would have rather dealt with an argument than to be completely ignored. Finally, I reached out and gripped his shoulder. I started to say his name, but the way Dominik jerked gave me pause. Had he really not noticed me standing there? The thought left me feeling empty, but I didn't dwell on it too long. Dominik's eyes flashed up to meet mine, and for an instant, I forgot how to breathe.

Those clear blue pools had returned. I couldn't remember the last time I had seen them, and I forgot how powerful they were. Diamonds would be jealous. I swallowed and smiled, "Are you ready to practice?"

Dominik frowned and bobbed his head forward and back, forward and back. It was a slow and careless movement, one which caused his hair to drift about his head.

"Yes, but on one condition."

My stomach twisted into a knot.

"What condition?"

His frown lifted at the corners to reveal a smirk.

Though my shoulders dipped back down to relax, my mind was still reeling from the intensity of his stare. I didn't think I could handle any more surprises, especially if it required me to make any decisions. I wasn't very good at making decisions. It took a lot of effort to make my lungs work properly, and my lips were drying more quickly than I could moisturize them.

Dominik smiled and said, "I want to play Die Lorelei."

I shook my head and crossed my arms, not because I didn't want to play it but because of my own absurd emotions. I had wasted panic over something as stupid as a request to play our song. Then I blushed. It was our song. I didn't say a word in response, expecting Dominik to move on his own accord. He sat firmly in place. I shot him a look, hoping he'd get the message and move over but he shook his head. Exasperated, I nearly growled, "How do you expect me to teach you when I can't even sit down?"

Dominik shook his head again and released a hearty laugh, one that bounced around the auditorium. It was a beautiful laugh, but it had my blood boiling. Whatever he had planned wasn't what I wanted, I was sure of that. It took Dominik a few minutes, laughing, wiping his eyes, laughing again and finishing it off with choked breaths to recover before he was able to respond to me. He said, "Who said I need teaching?"

It took me aback, and I shook my head. I couldn't believe it. "What do you mean?" I motioned towards the stand, "You already know the song?"

With a smug grin, he nodded. It was the happiest he had been for days, and while I was glad to see it, I was still confused.

"Okay. Then what am I supposed to do?"

He didn't say anything, but his eyes shifted pointedly above my shoulder. I didn't have to check to know what he was looking at. I swept the strap of the violin case off my shoulder and held it out in front of me. I met Dominik's eyes and he nodded. He wanted me to play my violin. My palms became moist beneath the fabric as I ran my fingers up and down the locks of the case. I hadn't played the violin in so long, and the weight felt unnatural in my hands. I wanted to argue. I wanted to run away, but the longer I stood there with Dominik's eyes fixed on me, the more I wanted to play it. Not for Dominik, but for myself.

I turned around and set the case down on the floor. The locks squealed on their hinges, but they glided open as if I had done the same thing the day before. The violin was covered in a thin layer of gray dust, but even with that I could still see the individual grains of lacquered redwood. The bow snuggled up beside it, its hairs were frayed from previous use, but it was still just as beautiful as when I had last used it. I swiped a hand across the front, the sheen beneath greeting me with a flash of light. I found myself smiling, but I didn't try to hide it. I plucked the violin from the felt and cradled it close to my chest before pulling out the bow.

With both pressed to my front, I sprang to the front of the stage and held the instrument up. It was muscle memory, just like it was when I played the piano. My muscles warmed with memory as I pressed my chin into the rest and touched the bow to the strings with an added flourish. I could hear Dominik snickering in the background, and I snickered inside, too. I will admit, nothing is like playing the piano. It feels comfortable behind those ivory keys, where I can play and flourish without the prying eyes of the audience. The violin, on the other hand, feels vulnerable and free. As I held the violin in my hands, I felt open. It was strange and new, but I liked it. I turned back to look at Dominik. His hands stroked the keys in a pattern I was familiar with. It was the folk song. So he had been practicing. Something about the way he sat at the piano, poised and confident had my heart aching.

I shrugged my shoulders and said, "But I don't know the music on violin."

I was lying. I could transpose music in my sleep, and the jump from piano to violin was no problem for me. Yet I told Dominik the lie anyway. I couldn't be sure why, but it didn't matter. His gaze shifted to me, clear and seemingly all-knowing. He smiled and nodded in my direction.

"You'll figure it out. The violin suits you."

My face heated with a blush, and I turned to face the empty auditorium just to hide my reaction. My heart no longer ached. His confidence in me had my entire body warm, and I was sure I was glowing. I repositioned the bow, cleared my head and my throat, then counted off, "One, two, three."

I drug the bow across the strings, and their voices were young and vibrant. It was as if they hadn't aged a day. I closed my eyes, took in the sounds of my breathing and the sounds of the violin breathing along with me. It was a beautiful harmony I had failed to recognize all those years ago when I switched from violin to piano. I missed it. I missed it more than words could express, so I let the music say it for me.

As I heard Dominik's staccato notes meld into my own melody, I allowed myself to open my eyes and scan the room. I imagined it full of people, faceless but lively. They sat quietly and focused on our performance, but there was someone particular I was looking for. My eyes grazed over the back row, nearly hidden in the darkness as a black smudge, but at the very center was the figure of a man I didn't recognize. He stood out among my imagined, faceless creations. He wore a brimmed military cap that hid the top half of his face from my view. My imagination was getting the best of me. I tried to pull my eyes away and go back to focusing on my music, but I couldn't bring myself to do it. I had to see his eyes. Whatever I was searching for, I would find it when my eyes met his, and as if he could read my thoughts, his face lifted. My eyes met a set of intense orbs. My immediate thought was of Dominik, but the eyes I met were not blue but green instead. The longer I lingered on those eyes, the more my imagination ran. Could that be Dominik's brother?

The thought shocked me. I hadn't prepared myself for such an intrusion, which distracted me from what I was playing. Where silence should have been, my note took hold and dragged on in a fading sweep. I froze, panting, and listening to the heavy silence that followed. Had the room actually been filled, I would have been mortified. Even though the room was empty, I felt mortified. I had made a mistake. What's worse, I had done it in front of Dominik. I would have rather messed up in front of an entire audience than during such an intimate performance. I had already begun preparing myself for a run when I heard Dominik take in a breath.

He didn't have a microphone, but he didn't need one. His voice hummed into the silence, hushed, before growing and filling the room with a chorus. It was beautiful. But his part on the piano took a turn, his piano part morphing into a lower version of the vocal part. He had been doing much more than practicing. I was grateful. It left me to do what I did best, a solo on the violin. We were taking so many liberties, and I loved it.

My hands quivered with fever and sweat as I scraped the bow across the strings, drawing out notes that were usually meant to be cut short. I cut notes which were meant to be drawn out. I was being nontraditional, and I was loving it. It was the freest I had ever been in my entire life. Dominik was rubbing off on me. But as we neared the end of the song, our instruments and his voice seemed to form one entity on their own accord. Three completely different sounds were tying in together and danced around the room. I loved it, and I wished such a sound could go on forever, but I found myself drawing my bow away. It was an achingly slow process, but it felt right. I allowed my own sound to fade away, leaving Dominik's piano and his humming voice to carry the rest of the song away to the end. As I listened, I allowed my eyes to slide shut and I lifted my face to bask in the light of the auditorium. That was how heaven felt.

Eventually, Dominik's voice tapered off on the last word and I basked in the echoing silence. It was in those moments of silence, when it was only mine and Dominik's thoughts left, that I dropped my bow to one side and my violin to the other. I loved Dominik. There was no denying it anymore. I loved him. I loved the way his voice cracked when he sang, I loved how angry he could make me, though I knew he didn't do it intentionally, I loved that he made me question myself and I loved just existing with him. I loved existing.

But just as I came to consider how I would tell him, the unnatural sound of applause cut through my most cherished silence. My eyes shot open and I jerked in the direction of the sound. Standing at the edge of the stage curtain, the head clapped and cheered. He was overjoyed. He was glowing with pride, but I was heating with anger. Our silence had been invaded and there would be no retrieving the moment. The head didn't pay any attention.

I turned back to see how Dominik was handling the situation, but he was hunched over the piano, taking in silent gasps. I hadn't realized how powerful his performance truly was. I flushed at the thought. I bet he looked beautiful, and while I was proud of my own performance, I was disappointed that I didn't get to see his performance. I was glad there hadn't been anyone to see it. I would've hated them. Then I remembered the head and felt all the more violated.

I met the head's eyes again and allowed a touch of my anger to spill from my lips. I asked, "Why are you here?"

The head paused in his joyous uproar, just long enough to mold a smile to his lips and to clasp his chubby hands in front of him. He didn't answer my question. I don't even think he was in the same room as us. He was somewhere else, thinking of other things. His eyes drifted between me and Dominik, Dominik and me, back and forth, back and forth. He was planning something, and my stomach told me that it wouldn't be good.

A few more awkward moments passed among the three of us before the head clapped his hands together, three times, as if to call us to attention. It was an aggravating display. He cleared his throat and opened his arms wide.

"Klemens, you've outdone yourself!"

Though what he said should have been taken as a compliment, its warm, rosy glow brushed right past me. I clenched my hand into a fist around my bow before I repeated my question, "What are you doing here?"

The head's mouth screwed up into a scowl. He looked offended. I tried to give him a look of my own, but it felt wrong against my features. He splayed his hands out in front of him, a martyr-like pose before he confessed, "I had to see how you were treating our new student." His eyes lighted on Dominik before he continued, "And my, oh my, you've done a fine job!"

I wondered if Dominik squirmed over his gushing as much as I did. It was beyond uncomfortable. He was keeping something back, skirting around the issue with praise and cheerful smiles. I was tired of the games, but held firm, settling for taking my anger out on the bow in my fist. The poor strings didn't deserve it, but I couldn't take out my anger on anything or anyone else.

The head, pleased with himself, strode toward the front of the stage where I stood. He eyed the violin in my hands and said, "I had no idea you could play the violin so well." His eyes flickered up to meet mine, and he smiled. "Seems the student has taught the teacher a few things as well."

I flushed and scowled. He was playing with me. Why he was, I couldn't decide. I suppose he just thought it was funny, but I wasn't laughing. If I hadn't been in my right mind, I would've beaten him with the bow of my violin. My Austrian roots wouldn't usually allow such an outpour of emotion, but after such an emotional performance, my nerves were already frazzled. I was much more inclined to follow my impulses. Finally, it seemed my silence had an effect. The head cleared his throat and fanned himself uselessly with his hands for a few moments before finally reaching into his coat pocket for a kerchief. I was extremely jealous.

He dabbed the piece of cloth to his forehead and around his neck, all the while clearing his throat. Once he had finished his preparations, he tucked the cloth back in his pocket and said, "Now, Klemens, I know you weren't so keen on having a partner in the beginning."

I grimaced. I had forgotten all about my old feelings toward performing with Dominik. I couldn't imagine my life without him. Oh, how things had changed. Noticing the shift, the head spluttered. "You may still be upset, but I swear, this has all led to much better things."

I maintained my grimace because I liked how it made the head squirm, but my eyebrow quirked on its own. He had me interested. He cleared his throat again and crossed his arms across his chest. I suppose that it was supposed to make him seem more concrete and serious, but he reminded me of a child about to throw a temper tantrum. The image lightened my mood, and I felt a bit better about hearing him out. I nodded for him to continue and he nodded back.

"Yes, well, because of your great work with Dominik, I would like to offer you a debut spot in the school's upcoming showcase."

For me, his offer relieved all the tension immediately, but the moment he went silent, I heard the scuffing of the piano stool and the quick, determined pace of Dominik. I tried to turn toward him, but he had made it to my side before I was even given a chance. Our shoulders brushed, and I started from the unexpected contact. I could feel my face start to heat up, but I did my best to focus only on the head and his offer. His eyes went back and forth between us, his syrupy smile creeping back onto his face.

"Think about it as Dominik's big debut in the school, and your debut on the violin. I firmly believe it will be the performance of the year."

I nodded, absorbing every word with enthusiasm. I finally did it. I had proven myself on the violin, and I would be able to share it with Dominik. My eyes drifted to where our arms touched, and I found that our hands were nearly together. *What would it be like to hold his hand?* I wondered. I began to brush my fingers against his when his hand jerked and locked into a fist. I jumped, but didn't say anything. I looked back to the head and found him staring at our hands, a look of confusion twisting his face. I blushed and locked my gaze onto him, though I tried to get a glimpse at Dominik's face. I couldn't see him well enough. My stomach was beginning to sour again.

I tried to focus on the news and the possibilities such an honor would present, but I couldn't seem to shake the lingering need to see Dominik's face. "Thank you. We would love to perform."

I barely caught Dominik's wild jerk as I spoke, but the head was already clapping again before I could ask him if he was okay. The head was giggling and rattling off a list of things that needed to be done, though most seemed like things that only he could do.

"Wonderful, wonderful. Your families need to be contacted, they will be sent tickets to attend, you will need to submit a set list to my office by the end of this month so we can prepare for the performance in March." He clutched his belly and let out a hardy laugh. "Isn't this just exciting?"

The head didn't give us a chance to answer, and continued to rattle off his lists as he waddled out the backstage exit and disappeared from our view. Once again, we were alone, but the mood had changed. The silence was no longer intimate or welcome. It had soured right along with my stomach, and I thought I was developing an ulcer. I turned to face Dominik and found his gaze already fully trained on me. It was unnerving.

My mind reeled with questions, but the only thing I could manage to say was, "March is only two months away."

It was the wrong thing to say. Dominik aged right before my eyes. His skin seemed to wilt and crease in places only my grandparents had, and his blue eyes clouded. It made him look like he had cataracts. My heart ached just thinking about such a thing. I wanted to ask what was wrong, how he was feeling, why he was feeling that way, but all I could do was splay my hands out in front of me, like a martyr. I hated myself for that. Dominik tilted his head to the side and smiled, shaking his head back and forth.

He let out a deep chuckle before stating, in a stale monotone, "Of all the people in the world, Klem, I figured you'd be the one to know better."

The heat in my chest was spreading up through my neck and into my face. It was so abrupt and intense, I couldn't decide if I was going to puke or cry. Probably both. My hands shook as I gripped the front of my shirt, as if it would make the heat stop, but it didn't. When had I started sweating? It didn't matter. None of it mattered. All I needed to know was the one thing Dominik wouldn't tell me. How was I supposed to make it better if he didn't tell me? I was going to have another panic attack. There was no way my heart could take much more of this stress.

But Dominik didn't keep me wondering long, "Did you even think to ask if I wanted to perform?" he nearly growled as he went back to the piano and began to put up the music. I was left watching him, stunned into silence and emptiness.

He didn't leave it there, either. He continued, "You

were the only one to ask when others thought I couldn't speak English, but I am suddenly invisible to you the moment you get a chance to shine."

I tried to retaliate, but there was nothing to say. I had no way to counter him, and as he finished up his imitations at normalcy and turned back to face me, I knew everything he had said was true. I had hurt him, more than any other had because he thought I wasn't like those people. Why had I been so hurried in accepting such a stupid performance? But the emptiness, left to burn, was like fire in my chest, and created words for me. Words I still regret.

"Why do you get to decide whether we perform or not? Didn't I work hard for this? What was the point in all of this if I don't get to at least do what I love?"

Dominik didn't look surprised, taken aback, or any more hurt than he already was. His face fell into a blank slate, and the blanket of silence was broken by the sound of his shoes as he squeaked across the stage. He passed me without touching and headed straight toward the backstage entrance. I followed him with my eyes, the anger still burning hot and heavy in my chest and throat. I wanted answers. I wanted him to answer me. I wanted him to yell and scream too, but he didn't. He made it all the way to the door, opened it enough so he could squeeze through, paused, then looked back and said, "Who said I would've said 'no'? You see me like all the others do – you don't see me at all."

He slipped through the door and disappeared. The hot coals inside me simmered and burned, leaving me more scorched than I had been before. All he had wanted was to be included.

6 – THE TRIO

Our practices afterword were stifled to the point where I would leave gasping for breath all the way home. It was suffocating and painful. We no longer except to change pieces, and even that was stilted, awkward and just unpleasant in general. I longed for the days before. I would've even preferred the anger and the arguments. At least we would have had some regular human interaction. I missed interacting, and I didn't even try to mention the folk song. If there was ever a song I wanted to avoid, it was that one. Yet I was inexplicably drawn to it. I wanted to go back so badly, I was willing to risk an awkward fight to get there.

Regardless of what my heart was telling me to do, my head kept me silent. We instead focused all of our efforts on songs that he could learn on the piano and sing to, while I played on the violin. The first time I had played the violin, I had never felt so free, so close to myself, so close to Dominik, and now I was back to being alone when I played. I might as well have been standing at the end of the stage, silent and alone with the room filled to the brim. It was how I felt. Still, the music was perfect. We played it with just as much skill as we had before, but it sounded empty – as empty as I felt. We were just playing what was on the page, and it hurt.

But eventually, we had to face the pain head on, and it was the day I had to turn the set list in. We had to end practice early just so I could stew over it. I had been putting it off for weeks, but the head made sure to call me before the school even opened and left me a voicemail, telling me that I needed to have it turned in by the end of the day. I couldn't put it off any longer, much to my dismay.

I brought the topic up to Dominik as he sat idly at the piano, but he just looked at me and scooted down the piano stool to give me room. I huffed and wanted to say something to him. I ended up just sitting down. It had been so long since we shared the stool together, it felt strange and inappropriate. Yet, I could still remember the days it had felt intimate and close. Like we were meant to sit on the stool together. I missed those days, so much.

I tried to imagine everything was normal, or that I was at least at the piano by myself, but Dominik's heat was too close to ignore. Still, I pulled the piano cover down to create a makeshift desk and began to scribble what I hoped would be a decent set list. An impromptu performance usually required six polished pieces, and we had only five in our repertoire. It wasn't a perfect list, but it would be enough to get us by. When I stopped and looked at the list, I realized that I didn't want just sufficient. I wanted perfection. I wanted to bring back the perfection and music our practices had and put into the performance we would have.

My eyes casually drifted over to Dominik. His eyes were glued to the set list, and I wondered if he was thinking about the same things I was. Did he want it all back? Or was he regretting ever meeting me? My own self-loathing aside, I didn't think Dominik hated me. He was not the kind of person who held grudges, or, at least, I didn't think he was. I was not sure about anything anymore, but I tried to believe in Dominik. I tried to believe in who I thought Dominik was, and as I thought about him, I tried to picture the performance. As it droned on through the first five pieces, the finale, the brightest spot of all the showing, was Die Lorelei, just as it should be.

I didn't snap back to reality until Dominik's finger thumped against the paper. I jumped and immediately regretted it as he cowed back to his side of the stool. I pressed my hand flat on the page, my fingertips brushing the sixth line where the heat of Dominik's hand seemed to linger. I wanted to revel in the feeling, but tried to play it off as flattening the paper instead. My voice was painfully stifled in my throat as I tried to find the words to ask him about the German folk song, but they just wouldn't come to me. Thankfully, Dominik spared me again.

His accent was much thicker than usual, just as it had been when we first spoke to each other. He nearly growled, "The folk song. We should end it with the folk song."

I smiled in spite of myself.

"Are you sure?" my questioning was weak, just a poor attempt at reasoning with him, trying to include him in the process, which I hadn't done before. But I was so excited about his suggestion, my cheeks ached from my smiling. Yet, I continued to question. I needed more confirmation.

"We haven't practiced it in a while. It might not be our best anymore." I winced at the final statement, and I prayed he didn't actually believe what I was saying.

Dominik met my gaze and smiled, though it was a defeated kind of smile. The kind of smile that pulls at the corners of your mouth, as if it is too much effort. He looked defeated, and it hurt me to think that he actually agreed with what I had said. I wanted to kick myself, but I doubted I would have the strength necessary to do it properly. I must've worn my emotions on my face. He shook his head and gave me a smile, one of his real smiles. Then he lifted his hand and brushed the fingertips across my left cheek. I hadn't realized that I was crying until his dry fingers pressed in and soaked up the tears.

I flushed at the thought of my pitiful show in front of Dominik, but he didn't look worried or perturbed. He smiled and trailed his fingers up from my cheek to my ear until the palm pressed gently against my cheek. He was warm, much warmer than I had ever imagined before. The close contact had me frozen in place, though I also didn't want to shy him away again. I loved Dominik's warmth.

Dominik shook his head and made soft cooing noises. It made me feel foolish, like being comforted as a young child, but I loved the way he stroked my cheek with the palm of his hand and used his other hand to resettle the glasses on my face. They had begun to fog and slide from my face because of the tears. I couldn't believe I hadn't noticed. I blamed it on the thrumming of my heart in my chest, in my face, and in my ears. I was thrumming all over.

He was muttering something, a mix of English and German. It sounded like a lullaby, but spoken instead of sung, and it was beautiful. My eyes fluttered shut as I took in his words, though I didn't understand any of them. I didn't have to.

Then, he spoke and his words were much softer than they had been in the past couple of days, "What is wrong, liebe?"

His accent wasn't thick, but it wasn't light either. It was a natural sort of German, which slipped in at every syllable. Everything he said was music, and I wanted to revel in it as long as I could, just in case the Dominik who cooed and comforted me decided to disappear again. I shook my head, eyes still locked shut, though a blush had begun to cover my face again as he spoke the word "liebe." I didn't know much German, but I knew that word.

The German word for love. Its presence hung in the

air around us, and I felt the urge to tell him. To tell him everything, everything about my feelings, my confusion, my love for him, which I still couldn't explain. It lurked at the tip of my tongue, begging to spill forth and to live free within the confines of our little world. But I couldn't get the words out. I only sobbed, and Dominik's hands dropped from my face to my shoulders. He tugged on them, but didn't have to do much before I was falling into his arms and burying my face into his collarbone. It was the closest we had ever been, and Dominik took it in stride.

He stroked my hair and fiddled with the collar of my shirt, while I clutched, like a child, onto him and cried. My glasses were fogged and pressed against my eyes and nose so painfully, but I couldn't bring myself to move away. My arms wrapped around Dominik almost perfectly, though I was surprised to find him so muscular. Did he work out or was he naturally toned? The thought had me stumbling internally. There was no doubt I would be embarrassed about all of this later, but at the moment I was happy.

Dominik never said a word as I shook in his arms. He was just there, which was all I really wanted. No. It was what I needed. What I wanted was something more, but I couldn't bring myself to ask. It was enough for him to just hold me and comfort me, to let me know that even though things were bad, they were going to get better. I didn't know if he was still mad at me or not. I was just grateful for him.

I lifted my face out of his shirt, just enough so my eyes peered at his shoulder and my cheek pressed against his neck. He smelled wonderful. How had I never noticed? It was like the beach. I felt a strange calm rest over my body. The thrumming stopped, the tears ceased, but my breathing grew deeper and more labored. Then, it hit me. A strange heat spread from my face, to my chest, down into my stomach, and even further down. Was I getting turned on?

Why then? Why did it have to be right then when I was pressed so close against him? I squirmed and tried to move about, but I only managed to make him squeeze me tighter. I groaned inwardly and prayed he didn't notice, though the longer we remained in that position, the worse off I was. Eventually, though I hated to break our perfect moment, I had to speak. I had to save myself from complete embarrassment.

"Dominik, I-"

But the grumble in his chest stopped me. Without saying a word, he pushed me back into a sitting position and I gasped at the sudden change in temperature. He was so warm, and being separated from him froze me to the core. Yet, the way his eyes locked on to mine helped to hold the memory of his heat. I swallowed my nerves as his hands traveled up from my shoulders, to my neck, to again cup my face, though this hold was much different than the comforting one.

I held his gaze the entire time, his eyes clear and open. His eyelids dipped until they shaded his eyes, and his body leaned toward mine until our noses touched and the heat of his breath warmed my lips. I couldn't speak, I couldn't breathe, I just held my body still, though my eyes closed on their own accord. I listened as precisely as I could to him, the rustling of his clothes as he squirmed, the heavy increase of his breath, then his lips brushed against mine. It was just a touch at first, a timid test, but I wanted more. So did Dominik.

Our lips touched, then they locked, and the rest of practice was spent on the piano stool, exploring, enjoying, and existing as one person created through a joining of lips.

We eventually left the music hall, much to my chagrin. I could've gone on for hours, but any longer and we would've spent the entire night in the school building. Dominik made up for it though. As we made our way out of the building, he held my hand in his, playing with my fingers and exploring the indents between my knuckles. It was a simple motion, but it had my heart soaring. We didn't speak. I didn't think we needed to. What words could express how I felt? I had never felt like that before, and I didn't want to ever stop feeling like that, like I was in love.

We did have to part as we headed toward our separate living quarters, but not without getting a final goodnight kiss, then a reminder of our future practices. As I walked alone in the dark, all I could think about was how heavy my heart was, and how I had never been more eager to carry it in my life. I wondered if Dominik was thinking the same thing.

7 – THE HARMONY

Our days progressed rather smoothly after that. Every day we played and practiced, especially Die Lorelei, which the head was pleased to find, was the finale to our performance. But something was amiss in the world we had built of music and long kisses. Dominik was reserved, and he had been growing progressively more so as the performance grew closer and closer. Soon, deep and intimate became quick and fleeting, and I found myself questioning us all over again.

I wanted to talk it over with him, to give us a chance and make us better, but every time I tried to bring it up, he would look at me and those eyes just pulled me in. Why waste a perfect moment for kissing with words that could be spoken at any time? And in all honesty, I still didn't know what our relationship really was. I could say, without a doubt, that I was completely in love with him. He was everything I wanted and more, and I would tell him in a heartbeat if he ever asked. But that was the thing. He never did ask. Not only did he never ask, but he never expressed one way or the other how he felt. I suppose I was just as guilty. I had never told him outright how I felt, but I couldn't get over the uncertainty of it all. Why hadn't he said anything yet?

I always tried to brush of such thoughts with thoughts of our future performance, of seeing my family and introducing him as my boyfriend. I smiled to myself at the idea. The thought of their surprise and terror filled me with absolute glee, which often had me randomly giggling to myself for no reason at all. I knew Bernard would be happy for me. He would be happy no matter what I decided. His love was one I could always count on. But even though that made me warm with happiness, the thought of Dominik slipped back in. Could I always count on Dominik's love? Did Dominik love me?

The closer we got to the performance day, the farther away I hoped that such thoughts and questions would be, but that was never the case. A week before the performance, I found myself more worried about my love life than my very public, very advertised and very important duet. I was fumbling on Die Lorelei. How was I messing up on that song, of all things. For the fifth time, Dominik called me over to the piano. I begrudgingly stomped my way over to him, heated and angry from my constant mistakes. He had been performing perfectly, I was the one messing up. Despite my love for him, I found myself growing extremely jealous of his ability to perform so easily. Maybe he really wasn't in love with me. I clenched the bow of my violin.

My anger must've shown, because Dominik's face scrunched up into worry, and I found my anger growing cold the longer he looked at me like that. Emptied of such heavy emotions, I let out a groan and pinched the bridge of my nose, careful not stab myself with the bow at the same time.

"Liebe, what is on your mind?" I had grown accustomed to his German accent, and found that he sounded unnatural without it. Hearing it then only managed to make me regret ever being angry at him.

I shook my head. I didn't want to talk about it anymore. Dominik shook his head and patted the empty part of the bench beside him. He wasn't going to let me get away that easily, and I wasn't going to fight him on it. With a sigh, I sat down, careful to keep myself distant from him, at least where we didn't touch. I don't think I could've handled it. But it didn't matter what distance I put between us, Dominik closed the gap just as quickly as I made it. He leaned toward me and pressed a heated kiss to my cheek – just a peck. Nothing compared to the kisses we had shared before. Then he drooped his head until it rested firmly against my shoulder. Without thinking, I shifted the bow into my other hand with the violin, then draped an arm around his shoulders, shifting his head a bit more onto my chest. I wondered if he could hear my heart thrumming. I hoped not.

The way he slumped against me was nice, warm and comforting, but I couldn't help feeling as if there was something more. The way he lay there, silent and unmoving, like a statue. It wasn't like Dominik. He always seemed fluid to me, always changing, and the fact that he was so still spoke volumes.

His shoulders heaved with a sigh before he spoke, and his voice weighed more on me than he did on my shoulder.

"Klem, I have to tell you something." He paused, taking in another breath before adding, "Soon."

We sat in silence for a little while as I let the words hang in the air. I worked myself up to ask him why we had to wait, but I never got the chance. Just as I opened my mouth to ask, the doors to the auditorium flew open, much louder and harder than I could ever recall. My gaze shot over to the door and Dominik ripped himself from my arms, I didn't take the time to look at him, instead glancing at the man who marched as a smudge through the darkened seats. I tried to shade my eyes from the light to get a better look, but it didn't help.

The man was rigid and his stride was more of a march than a regular walk. I saw the military uniform before I saw his face, as the shining medals and brightly colored bars caught the light from the stage. Dominik rose from the stool and marched himself to the edge of the stage, though his posture was lacking when compared to the man who stopped and saluted him. Dominik saluted back.

I remained silent as the performance took place. I couldn't speak, I couldn't ask questions, it all seemed too delicate and official for me to intervene. I felt odd, out of place, though I also felt invaded. This was my stage, my auditorium, and as I watched Dominik lower his hand from his brow to his side, mechanically and precisely, I couldn't help but think that he was *my* Dominik, too. I had to lean back to see around Dominik and to finally glimpse the man's face. His mouth was screwed up in the ugliest of scowls, forming lines of anger and disappointment. His eyes were trained on Dominik's face, and he did nothing but lower his hand away and mutter something that made Dominik wince. I think it was, "At ease."

It didn't hit me until his green eyes latched onto me. It was his brother. That was Dominik's brother. I physically jerked as my brain made the connection, and I found myself struggling to keep balanced as I settled back onto the bench and comfortably hid behind Dominik. My nerves were absolutely shot. I looked to Dominik, but he had no answers to give. He peered back to me and tensed as he remained completely still and clenched. I heard something said in German, but I didn't have time to mull it over before my cover moved from his position, allowing his brother to lock eyes with me again.

Dominik met my eyes for a brief instant, and I caught a slight hint of guilt along with an unspoken apology. I wanted to ask him why he would apologize, but my thoughts were stifled as his brother gave me a smile. It was stiff and insincere, almost condescending in the way only one side quirked while the other lay slack. For a man with perfect posture, he seemed extremely crooked. While he smiled, his eyes roved up and down my face and my body, and I found myself stiffening up and straightening my clothes for no real reason. My face heated up, but I did my best to remain still.

Finally, Dominik's brother looked me straight in the eyes again. His smile failed for only an instant, but it was quickly replaced by a much more enthusiastic grin, though it didn't quite meet his eyes.

"Brother, do not be rude. Introduce me to your," he paused to run his eyes up and down my face one more time, then continued with an emphasized, "*friend*."

I looked to Dominik, trying to read some sign. He shrank in on himself, his shoulders dipping low and forward. He didn't meet my eyes. The fact that he didn't correct his brother or elaborate on our relationship brought up all of my previous insecurities. I tried my best to keep from slumping in on myself, too, but I felt myself crumbling. I prayed that his brother wouldn't stay long, but it didn't seem like I was going to get my way.

"Sven," he motioned toward his brother, then shifted his hand to me, "this is Klemens." He repeated the gesture in the opposite direction before continuing, "And Klemens, this is my brother, Sven."

His voice remained monotone the entire time, and his eyes were locked on the stage in front of him. It wasn't what I had come to know. This Dominik was someone completely new to me, and I didn't like him. Where was the Dominik who so confidently kissed me? Held me close and told me his true feelings? Who could play the violin with as much gusto, if not more, than Mozart himself, though he had only learned over a few months? He wasn't the man who stood before me now. He was somewhere far away, hidden behind a mask of fear and embarrassment.

As my anger grew, I decided if Dominik could act, I

could too. I put on my best smile as I stood up from the stool and made my way toward the end of the stage where Dominik stood. I caught Dominik's sharp and shocked gaze, a quick warning for me to stop, but I pretended not to see and continued my own march. Once at the end of the stage, I made a grand show of bowing before thrusting my arm toward Sven where I met his surprised gaze.

"It is nice to meet you," I cocked an eyebrow for effect before continuing, "General?"

Sven stared at my hand for a few seconds, then allowed his gaze to travel between Dominik and me. Then, he returned my smile and grasped my hand. It was a firm grasp, just as I had expected it would be. He didn't seem as enthusiastic as I acted, but he didn't seem cold either. He was just uncomfortable, but he remained stoic and went along with the formalities.

Sven cleared his throat and said, "Well, it seems my reputation precedes me." His gaze shifted back to Dominik, "I did not realize my little brother spoke of me."

I cut a gaze to Dominik, pleased to find his mouth gaping and his eyes wide with shock. His eyes met mine and he promptly shut his mouth before cutting me an awkward glare. I simply smiled and returned to Sven where I ended our handshake and straightened back up. I stood much taller than I ever had, much more confident than I had been in a while. It was nice to be the one in power, the one to make others squirm. I could feel the tension in the room beginning to rise as the silence drew out longer, and it would have been best to change the subject. I knew that. I could feel it, but I couldn't help myself. I wanted to make it go on for just a little longer.

I held a hand to my mouth, as if embarrassed, and said, "Of course, of course. I apologize for being so forward. I'm just surprised. With how much Dominik speaks of you, I can't believe I haven't met you yet."

It was in that moment, when my words fell away into the silence, that I knew I had gone too far. I had to cut my gaze back and forth between Sven and Dominik as their eyes locked. Neither one was going to move, and there was nothing I could do or say as the conversation became some sort of staring contest. It was a conversation I couldn't be a part of, and as I dropped the hand from my face, my skin began to heat as I realized how foolish I was. The silence was unbearable, and I was already trying to decide whether or not to bolt or to stay put when Sven suddenly shifted.

He straightened up and turned his face to look at me, though his gaze was still locked on Dominik as he said, "It was nice meeting you, Klemens, but I must be going." I looked to Dominik for a second, no longer surprised to find his gaze hidden by his hair, and his eyes trained on the ground. Sven continued, "Dominik, I will be at your dorm. Try to get in early."

It was supposed to be a suggestion, or at least it was fashioned to be one, but it sounded more like a command. Finally, Sven met my gaze, though he didn't even try to fake a smile, instead scowling as he saluted one last time, dropped his arms to his side, nodded another good-bye then marched out of the auditorium, just as he had when he arrived. As he exited, the room seemed to sag. It was as if his very presence had turned the entire room just as rigid as he was. But the calm didn't last.

Just as I was about to speak to Dominik, his eyes jerked in my direction, slitted and angry. His lips pulled tight across his lips, and every time he spoke it seemed more like a growl. "What was that about?"

I didn't need any clarification to know what he was talking about. I should have kept my mouth shut, and I wasn't going to make the mistake of opening it again. I remained silent, refusing to answer his question. It only seemed to anger Dominik even more. Exasperated, he scrubbed his face with his hands, then ruffled his hair over and over and over again. He was on the edge, and it seemed as if I was going to be the one who pushed him over.

He pinched the bridge of his nose, and that grounded him a bit, at least long enough for him to speak again. "What were you trying to achieve? What was going through your head?"

With every word, his voice grew in pitch. It was the angriest outburst I had ever seen from him, and it frightened me. Yet, a little voice in my head, an audible memory flickered into life. It was Sven's voice. Sven repeated over and over, "Friend." Was I really just a friend? Why did he get to be angry? I wanted to be angry, too. I wanted to yell and scream and demand answers.

"What am I to you?"

Dominik's mouth went slack. His brows furrowed as he thought, and I could see the wheels turning behind his eyes. He could only respond with, "What?"

A sigh clawed its way out of my throat as I gestured toward the piano, "We kiss, we talk, but it all started because of the music. Well, when the performance is over and the semester comes to an end, what then? Will you go back to Germany? Will you still talk to me? I want to know - no, I need to know. What am I to you?"

It all spilled out of me before I could filter it. All of my insecurities and questions were now out in the open, and as it came forth, with every new question, Dominik's face gradually went from surprise to a crumpled look of indifference. It was disappointing. I had at least hoped for compassion, but once I had finished, the indifference and silence wasn't hopeful. My heart lurched in my chest as I waited, but I refused to say anything else. I had to know what he was feeling before I could speak, otherwise, I wouldn't be able to keep it together.

Unfortunately, his response was no help. He stated, plain and monotone, "I always planned on going back to Germany."

That was it. That was the last thing he said to me. My heart felt as if it had fallen to my feet and rooted me to the floor. I froze and couldn't bring myself to move. My brain no longer functioned and neither did my body. I had never felt so numb before in my life. Dominik wasn't the least bit affected though, and he didn't act as if he noticed my distress. Either that or he didn't care. I guessed the latter of the two. He left me where I stood, picked up the music from the stand and put it back in place, moved all the equipment back to the storage area, then simply left. No good-bye, no words, he was just gone.

Alone, I repeated his final words out loud, "I always planned on going back to Germany."

Something about it was so final, such a painful good-bye. I'd never felt so hopeless before in my entire life.

8 – THE MELODY

Two days until the concert, Dominik and I were back on track, but we no longer kissed. He would peck my cheek once practice was over, but that was the extent of our intimacy. We were back to square one. It was terribly platonic, but I was at least able to play. It was never as intense or eye-catching as when Dominik and I had first started, but I had grown used to the on-again, off-again performances - much to my chagrin. Regardless, there was no time for questions or drama. It was all or nothing. Plus, it was impossible to continue our conversations with Sven now attending every practice. He would sit in the back row and just stare. I wasn't always sure who he was staring at, but it made me nervous. He always made sure to leave promptly 5 minutes before the practice was over, which allowed Dominik to give me his stale and routine good-bye.

Two days before the concert, Dominik was putting everything up, as usual, while I just watched. I didn't really do much of anything after practice anymore. What was the point? He never asked, and most of the time I had a bow and violin to care for, but the violin was perfect. No need for a polish or shine right before the performance. The sound had to stay as consistent as possible, up until after the concert, and it seemed that policy was being held by Dominik as well when it came to our relationship.

The comparison hurt my heart, and I clenched my violin tighter in my hand. It felt as if only my instrument understood me, and while it was a romantic notion, it managed to make me feel even more alone. There was no doubt in my mind that he would leave once the concert was over. He'd tell me good-bye with a handshake because his brother would be there. My only hope was that he would take the romantic approach and just disappear from my life. It would be the least painful, but the way my luck was going, I highly doubted that I would be so lucky.

It brought out a few tears, but I was far too used to wiping them away to care. I simply brushed a hand against my eyes and the tears were gone. I was about to skip the good-byes, cut them off before Dominik could do it himself, when the familiar squeal of the auditorium doors echoed throughout the room. My eyes drifted away from the violin case in my lap, and toward the back of the auditorium where I met a set of familiar brown eyes.

"Bernard?"

My brother, much shorter than the average teen, met me with a smile brighter than I had seen in days. His hair had grown much longer than I remembered, the black locks curling up to tickle the sides of his neck. What he lacked in height, he had gained in hair and personality. Bernard had always been reserved as a child, preferring the company of his paintbrush over that of our family, but as he bounded down the aisles, ignoring the stairs completely, and simply lunging up onto the stage, sprawled out at my feet, I realized just how much I had missed him. He looked up at me, a sheepish grin tugging at the corners of his lips.

"Brother. I have missed you."

His accent was much heavier in English, and it

reminded me of the time Dominik had put on his German accent. My heart lurched, but I did my best to smile back as I lent him a hand.

"Bernard. You have to be more careful."

Bernard took my hand with enthusiasm, and jumped up just as easily as he had lunged upon the stage. He was as vibrant as his paintings. As he stood before me, he brushed himself off, his bright smile drooping into an embarrassed frown. He was never one to take reprimands very well, even in jest, and Bernard was right back to the shy, reserved little boy I had left in Austria. It all left a bitter taste in my mouth, but I couldn't hold back the happiness at seeing a familiar face. Especially someone who truly loved me, too. I rested my hand on his shoulder, the closest thing to a hug my family allowed, and managed to pull back a shadow of the smile that had vanished.

"I will, brother."

Then, his eyes drifted away from me, and his head tilted along with them. I didn't have to turn my head to know who he was looking at. Dominik either didn't care or didn't pay attention. He didn't say a word, but Bernard refused to take his gaze off him. As much as I was glad to see my brother, I dreaded having to go back to the topic of Dominik. I wanted to talk to Bernard, free of any emotional pain and ties to Dominik. I wanted to talk about his paintings, about home, about our parents, anything. But that wasn't a viable option. I had to set aside my needs for a moment, and bring out the old Klemens; the Klemens who was proud of his Austrian heritage and as noble as a king. It would be best for all of us, and much tamer on my heart.

"Bernard, this is Dominik. He will be my partner for the concert. Dominik," and I feigned an attempt at cordiality when referencing him, but didn't pull it off as smoothly as I had intended, "this is my brother, Bernard."

Then, it occurred to me that Bernard was alone. There was no one around. No escort, no mother, no father. Hadn't they promised to attend? It wasn't like them to not show up without early notice.

"Bernard, where are mother and father?"

Bernard's face didn't hide a thing. His pixie features softened and relaxed, all except for the small muscles at the sides of his mouth, which tugged down into a frown. Whatever it was, it wasn't good news.

"I am sorry Klemens. Mother and father could not come. Mother had already promised to attend her friend's performance in Italy." His lips curled up, as if he had tasted something terrible. It almost made me laugh – almost. "It is an opera, and father had to escort her." All of the tension which had built up suddenly sagged. I was worried that he might cry, and I didn't think my heart could've handled that. "I am sorry. I begged for them to come along, but they refused."

My anger surged up my throat, scratching my voice into silence, but I swallowed it down as best I could. I wanted to scream, but my fear wouldn't allow it. The fear was something entirely new. Yes, my immediate reaction was indeed anger, but it wasn't over my parents' lack of interest in my performance. My first thought had been in another direction entirely. I had wanted them to come, not for my performance, but for Dominik. I had joked the entire time about introducing them and seeing the horror in their eyes, but some small part of me had hoped for their acceptance. If they met Dominik, would they accept him?

But why did it matter?

I had to physically shake myself to realize what I was doing, and it must have been all over my face, as Bernard was no longer looking around me. His brown eyes were trained on me, prying and studying everything that passed over my face. I felt vulnerable, but there was no hiding anything from Bernard. He wouldn't bring up his concerns in a public manner, but he wasn't going to let it go either. Instead, he directed his gaze back to Dominik, whose steps sounded heavy and flat as they echoed through the auditorium.

"It has been nice meeting you Bernard, but I have to be getting my rest. We have a big performance soon."

I envied Dominik. He could get out of anything without much effort. I either had to be blunt, or completely vague, and by the looks of Bernard's stare I would have to choose one or the other much sooner than I would have liked to. Dominik didn't help matters as his shoulder pressed against mine. I tried to avoid his gaze, instead turning my head to stare at his chest. Wrong choice, I realized all too late. He had recently started a ritual of white collared shirts and black pants. It would be what he performed in, and he believed in practicing the same way he would perform. His shirt was just as plain, white as always, but had he always unbuttoned the top two? I couldn't quite remember, but the heat in my cheeks didn't help matters. Trying to salvage what little dignity I had left, I shifted my gaze to his face, deciding it was the least dangerous part of him.

If I were a betting man, I would have lost. His bright eyes caught mine immediately, and his hand found the small of my back, familiar and confident. He dipped his head, hot breath trailing across my cheek and tickling my ear as he whispered. "I will see you tomorrow. Have a good night, Klemens."

Then, as always, he brought his mouth back to the apple of my cheek, though not without breathing another hot trail of his breath back across. He pressed his lips together and onto my skin, and when he finally did remove both hand and lips, he spared no time. He rushed out of the auditorium, rushing up the aisles in a pale blur, and his escape would've been completely silent if not for the heavy slam of the door as he disappeared behind it.

In the meantime, I froze in place. My breathing clenched in my lungs, and my chest heaved with every intake. Eventually, my breathing did ease, but the heat on my cheek and at my back lingered. I couldn't recall his touches burning as much as those.

But when I met my brother's eyes, my face burned just as powerfully as the touches. His mouth was open, eyes bugging from their sockets, and his hands were splayed outward in surprise. I swallowed as I realized that my decision had been made. Blunt was the only way to go, as if Dominik's actions hadn't been blunt enough.

It was weird sitting with Bernard at my dinner table. I lived on campus, and the dorms weren't necessarily the grandest of places, but my scholarships allowed me to have a single room. No roommate, less noise, and I could practice without the fear of interrupting another person's studying, at least in my own room. The neighbor's didn't complain. At least, they hadn't to my face.

Regardless, I usually dined alone. Silence, except for the occasional tap of silverware on my plates. It was my time for contemplation and relaxation, but with Bernard rudely scraping his food around into small piles, and his eyes drifting up to study me, like a specimen under a microscope, there would be no quiet self-reflection for me.

So, I placed my silverware to the side, opposite my napkin, which I picked up to pat my mouth. I dropped the napkin into my lap, and leaned back in my chair. My tafelspitz had gone cold a long time ago, and there would be no salvaging the dinner now. Anytime was as good as now to discuss everything and to both figuratively and literally put it all out on the table. Bernard watched me, dropping his own utensils right back on the plate with a clatter. I tried my best to not grit my teeth, but it was a lost cause.

As I tried to relax my building nerves, I thought for a moment how to broach the topic. Bernard was reserved, but he wasn't ignorant to the world. At the same time,

Bernard had only ever seen one person whom I had shared a romantic relationship with, and she was a woman. A bold woman, but a woman none the less. I tried to form an opening sentence, something both straightforward, but gentle, too. But my time was wasted. Bernard leaned forward, hands gripping the edge of the table.

"Why did you not tell me about your boyfriend?"

I opened my mouth to respond, but closed it just as quickly. It wasn't the question I had expected, not by a long shot, and my face heated up at the thought of Dominik being my boyfriend. Bernard's gaze remained locked on me, patiently waiting on my response, but I had no idea what to say. I tapped the edge of the table, which helped alleviate some of the nerves, though the sound didn't help. Unable to break the cycle of fear and annoyance, I decided to wing it. Surely I had something I could say. So, I opened my mouth and allowed the words to flow.

"He isn't my boyfriend."

Not the most eloquent of responses, but I was just glad to have formed a coherent sentence. Bernard slumped back in his chair, hands falling from the table. He gripped the sides of his chair, and I half wondered if he might launch from the table if he lost his grip, but he thankfully stayed put. His frown made my heart lurch in my chest, but my mind was spinning too fast for me to mourn over it for long. Why was Bernard so excited over this?

"Then why did he kiss you like that?"

I didn't know if I even had answer for that. Dominik had kissed me before, both on the lips and the cheek, but never with such heated passion. Even his touch had been on fire, and the thought still made my cheeks heat up.

"Klemens," Bernard squinted his eyes. "Are you hiding a scandal?"

If our parents were there, I probably would have been. I tried my best not scowl, but I'm not sure that I pulled it off, as Bernard physically wilted in his seat. I let out a sigh of frustration and scrubbed my face with the heel of my hand. I never thought I would ever have to go through this, mainly because I never thought I would fall in love while in school, much less with a German man. Then, I remembered that he was German, and after our concert he would be heading back to Germany, leaving me behind to finish my studies. Then I wilted into my chair.

I would finish within the next year, then go back to Austria where I would audition for a spot in different orchestras. My parents would be proud for a year, then complain when I didn't try for every solo available. I would travel the world, playing in the grandest of halls for the most eminent families in society, and I would retire to an estate that my parents would probably leave me. I would be wealthy, and completely alone. That single fact, despite the wonderful advantages of such a lifestyle, took the breath right from my lungs in a single rush. I pressed a hand against my chest to try to calm my rushing heart.

"Bernard, Dominik is from Germany. He'll be leaving as soon as the concert is over. We're just friends."

Bernard shook his head, cheeks tinted with his frustration. "You did not look like friends to me, and love can travel long distances."

I shook my head, holding back the bitter giggles that I felt. Bernard was too innocent to understand things like love. I couldn't recall him ever expressing any interest in love affairs to begin with, much less providing advice.

"I don't think you understand things like this-"

I wasn't given the chance to finish my sentence as Bernard rose from his seat and slammed his hands on the table, "You loved Elizaveta, and she resided in Hungary."

I shook my head, "Bernard, I loved her for a time, but that didn't work out-"

He interrupted me again, shaking his head furiously, and making his curls bounce around the frame of his face. I tried to understand his passion for this topic, but the hint of tears at the corners of his eyes made it hard to think through.

"Klemens, you have been in America for a long time, and I still love you. Did you not still love me while you were here?"

Then, I understood. Bernard had missed me more than I ever imagined. It had never occurred to me before, but as the tears slipped down his cheeks and his lips quivered, I couldn't imagine how I had never thought about it before. I stood up from my seat and rushed to his side of the table where, without much thought, I grabbed him and took him into my arms.

He froze, not used to physical contact, which hurt me even more than his tears. How had I gone so long without hugging him before? Eventually, he relaxed, and I began to feel the warm dampening of his tears against my shirt. His arms went around my waist and he cried. For how long, I couldn't be sure, but he did until he couldn't cry anymore. Then, I took him to my room to sleep, while I stayed on the couch, and then it was my turn to cry.

9 – THE FINALE

The next morning, I took the day off to show Bernard around the campus and the town. He had never had pizza before, and while I didn't care for the American version, it was well worth watching my brother scarf down piece after piece with a ferocity I had never seen. It might have been a mistake cancelling practice right before the concert, and my parents would be horrified if they ever found out. But I was confident in my ability then, and I am still confident in it now. I would be lying if I didn't admit, even after enjoying a day with my brother, that my mind kept going back to that auditorium. I wondered if Dominik had gone to practice anyway, and if his brother towered over him at the piano, mocking every missed note or fumbled hand position. Would his brother even allow him to practice without me there? Or was he completely alone? Something about the image of Dominik alone at the piano, singing his folk song as he pecked at the piano keys, depressed me even more than the image of his brother hovering over him.

Dominik reminded me a lot of Bernard. He wasn't as innocent and childish as Bernard, but he was just as reserved. Did he feel as alone as Bernard? Did he even feel alone when he was at home with his brother and parents? I couldn't decide one way or the other, but I was sure loneliness wasn't an uncommon feeling for Dominik.

I wondered if I had ever made him feel alone. The thought brought sorrow to my eyes, and I could feel the tears tickling the corners of my eyes, but the thought refused to leave. Instead, I focused on the concert, but that only managed to remind me that Dominik would be leaving me. Leaving me for Germany, while I was left wondering what we truly meant to each other for the little bit of time that we might have meant something.

While I understood what Bernard told me about love, I wasn't sure if what Dominik and I had between us was strong enough to withstand separation. What if? What if he was another Elizaveta? What would my parents say? That was another problem to contend with if we even stayed together. My parents were always on the search for my wife. They wanted grandchildren to carry on the name, one way or another, and that kind of arranged marriage wasn't unheard of in my parents' social circles. They were the least of my worries, though. I wouldn't have to see them again for another year, which was when I finished my studies.

Still, as I prepared for the concert the next day, white shirt buttoned up to the collar, and black pants, my mind was muddled with these questions and thoughts. The only thing grounding me was the sound of people behind the red curtain. It was a full house, except for four seats, which I took note of as I came in with Bernard. Both seats on either side of him were empty, which was where my parents would be had they attended. He didn't seem a bit bothered by the emptiness when I left him, but as I peeked out from behind the curtain, I couldn't help taking note of the nervous twiddling of his thumbs, and the jittery sway of his feet. Only two seats away sat Dominik's brother, Sven. His posture was absolutely superb, but rigid as usual.

He didn't look as if he wanted to be there at all, but both seats on either side of him were empty, too, and I took a bit of comfort in that.

Then, a hand brushed my shoulder, and I responded with a swift release of the curtain, flipping around to come face to face with Dominik. He neither smiled nor frowned, but his blue eyes danced and shone, even in the dimness of the backstage. They were clear, nearly see-through, and the longer I stared the more I thought I could see completely through him. I had to steady my breathing before I could speak, but it still came out with a stutter.

"H-hey, Dominik."

Dominik gave me a genuine smile, "Hey, Klemens. Are you ready for the spotlight?"

I swallowed the lump that had risen to my throat. I had performed in plenty of halls much larger than this, yet, I feared this performance the most, but I couldn't be sure why. A heat rose to my cheeks, and I found my thoughts drifting to things other than the concert, namely, Dominik leaving. It was then that I realized, I was not nervous about the performance. I could have been performing for royalty, and I wouldn't have batted an eyelash. What I feared was letting Dominik go without knowing what could be and what we were, at least in my eyes. The tears had begun to rise again, and I tried to hold them back, but it was too late. Dominik saw them.

He raised a pale hand to my face and brushed his thumb over my bottom eyelid, taking my tears with it and making his thumb shimmer. I wanted to apologize, but I thought it would be silly. Instead, when I opened my mouth to speak, no apology came forth. Instead, in a slow, aching whisper, my soul spilled forth.

"Dominik, am I your boyfriend? Or nothing at all? Do you love me? I can't let you leave without knowing. I can't imagine watching you go, leaving me alone with those unexplained kisses."

I waited, silent. I expected rejection, then I expected

immediate acceptance. I'm not sure what I expected anymore, my mind was flitting from one possibility to another, but what I didn't expect was laughing. And that's just what Dominik did. He laughed, and the heat in my cheeks changed into a sweltering inferno. But before I could scream and reprimand him, Dominik cupped my face in his hands, chilling me with his cooling touch.

"Klemens. When will you get the stick out of your ass?"

This shocked me again, but he gave me no time to process it all as he shook his head and continued his explanation.

"Why do we always have to say things out loud? Weren't my kisses enough to tell you?"

I began to shake my head in response, but his eyes locked with mine and caused me to go still again. He had never looked more serious. His eyes no longer shimmered, but became much more still and constant.

"Klemens. Always prim and proper." He pulled my face closer to his, brushing his lips against mine, "I love you."

Our lips locked, much more desperately than I could remember. It was like a lightning strike at midnight, when the light flashes and you question whether it was actually daylight or not. That immediate shock to the senses. That was what kissing Dominik felt like. Silent and bright, much like Dominik really was, the Dominik I had come to know and love in such a short time.

But as our kiss dwindled, I began to notice that the brightness didn't come just from his kiss. My eyelids were much more illuminated than before. The silence wasn't just in my mind either. Wasn't the crowd talking just a few moments ago?

I opened my eyes once Dominik broke our connection, only to see him completely brightened by the blue light I had requested for our performance. I was momentarily reminded of his angel wings, but only for a moment, as the smirk on his face and the rising tint of red on his cheeks reminded me there was much more to him than what meets the eye. I turned slowly to face what had been curtains, and was now a crowd of shocked faces, excluding Bernard, who sat smiling in the front seat. Sven, on the other hand, was shooting daggers in my direction. I had never seen the military man blush, and I didn't think he was capable of such a feat, but there he was, arms locked across his chest and his pale cheeks obviously red despite the dim light of the crowd.

I studied everyone's face, my own face flushed, unsure of how to go about moving forward. I heard the sound of someone trying to get my attention, and I shifted my gaze to the stage exit where the head was shooting his own set of daggers at me and Dominik. He motioned toward the piano and my violin at the front of the stage, but I couldn't bring myself to move. I wasn't embarrassed, much to my own surprise. If anything, I was frozen in a state of euphoria. I could still taste Dominik's lips on mine, and I didn't want it to disappear, not yet. But when I felt his hand at the small of my back, and his heated breath on my ear, ushering me to the piano, it was like flipping a switch. I steadied myself, and with all the confidence in the world, I made my way to the piano.

I took my usual seat, opening the music booklet on the stand to our first piece, then set my hands on the piano keys. I kept my gaze on the music, but could just make out Dominik's silvery-form as he positioned himself next to my violin and behind the microphone. I held down the middle C, and Dominik hummed back in response. We were in tune, perfect.

There was an uncomfortable murmur in the audience, then everyone settled back into silence. With my senses renewed, I began the count off for our first number, then faded into my music. No, not my music. It was *our* music.

Die Lorelei was by far the best song I had performed in my entire life, and the last one I would ever perform with my violin. The strings had never felt so alive, nor had they ever cried as heavily as when Dominik sang to them. His voice and my instrument were not the only ones who cried. When his voice broke with end of my violin's sound, I opened my eyes and peered out. People rose from their seats, applauding with passion and enthusiasm. My brother did not stand, his face hidden behind his hands as his dainty shoulders shook with sobs. Sven stood, but his face remained completely blank.

I locked eyes with him for an instant, but he only shook his head and disappeared into the back of the auditorium. I could only assume that he had left, and it only bettered my mood. The head rushed out to take my hand, and I struggled to grip with the bow still tight in my fingers. His eyes drifted over to someone beside me, and I immediately felt Dominik's warm fingers intertwining with mine. I ignored the head's gushing and put all of my focus on Dominik. He smiled, all teeth, and he absolutely shone beneath the blue lighting.

"Be proud, Mr. Austrian. You've outdone yourself."

I shook my head and smiled back, this time pulling it off as smoothly as he did.

"It's only because I had you with me."

Then, he blushed. A true, embarrassed blush. I laughed and turned back to face the crowd, then squeezed his hand and pulled him down with me into a bow. It was the performance of a lifetime.

10 - EPILOGUE

There was something sad about packing things into a box that I had only just seen. They were small glimpses into Dominik's life. Family photos, works of poetry he had written, CDs of both rock and classical German bands, and even a few sketches he had hidden away in the back of his desk. Such small glimpses, glimpses that I wish I could have delved into and explored more, but I only had a few hours left with him. We spent most of them kissing and tumbling around his apartment, despite all of the boxes and missing furniture. The rest was spent introducing Dominik to Bernard, and Bernard begged for him to teach him some German.

I let them have their fun while I resigned myself to his study where he still needed things packed. It gave me time to think, which led to my need to snoop. I snooped and snooped. There was hardly anything in English, and the only things worth noting were the sketches. Some made no sense to me when I found them, then I'd catch details. Fingers on piano keys, fingers pushing up glasses on a pair of detailed eyes, and hands fixing the strings of a violin. All of those hands were mine. As I thought of it, it reminded me of when I had seen Dominik's hands draped across the piano. I loved his hands then, and I loved his hands even more as I was preparing for the inevitable good-bye. It made my cheeks warm with the realization that he might have loved my hands, too.

I was all-engrossed in that thought. So much so that I never heard Dominik's footsteps as he walked up behind me. I sat on the carpet, legs tucked neatly underneath me while I pawed through the things I had just stuck in the single box. One box was enough to clear out the entire room, which filled me with an unexplainable sadness. How could so much personality and such a wonderful person fit into a single box? I couldn't dwell on it too long, as Dominik's hands rested on my shoulders and I felt him press his chest into my back as he sat down. His legs went out on either side of me, but his head wasn't high enough to reach my shoulder.

"Even by yourself you're prim and proper."

I scowled to myself and huffed, but I repositioned myself all the same. I was not new to relaxation, but never while entangled in the arms of another person. It was almost embarrassing how small I felt as Dominik's head rested on my shoulder and his arms draped across my chest. My legs stretched out parallel to his, but they were nowhere near as long. I awkwardly held his arms with my hands, but he didn't seem to mind. I wanted to revel in the feeling – the feeling of just existing with another person, but the thoughts still crept in. It was the last time I would be this way with Dominik until I went back to Europe. I didn't want to ruin the moment, but my voice clawed its way out anyway.

"What are we going to do?"

I didn't need to clarify. Dominik knew what I was referring to, and by the gradual heave of his chest as he sighed, I could tell he'd been waiting for me to ask.

"Klemens, you're going to do what you want to do while I'm gone, but I'll always be in Germany. When you join your esteemed orchestra and start traveling the country, I will find you. When you come to Germany and play all the solos, I will be sitting front row."

I turned to face him, breaking our wonderful position, but seeing his eyes, gleaming with emotion, made it all worth it.

"But how will you know? What if you forget about me?"

Dominik laughed, shaking his head.

"Klemens. Music is my life, and I know it's yours, too. Where there is music, I know I will always find you."

And with nothing else needing to be said, Dominik dipped his head low and pressed a kiss to my lips. I closed my eyes, and I kissed him back.

ABOUT THE AUTHOR

Alyssa Hubbard is an author to HUMANS AND THEIR CREATIONS and the APOCALYPTIA series. She was born in a small town in Alabama, where she spent more time writing and reading than playing outside. Her sister is a two-time cancer survivor, and she is her greatest inspiration. She attends the University of Alabama for a BA in English with a minor in Creative Writing. Alyssa spends most of her time reading, writing, re-writing, and re-writing, and re-writing, and re-writing... She loves blogging and singing in public.

For book teasers, information on future books, and general information on Alyssa Hubbard's crazy life, head on over to her website:

www.lissywrites.com

Follow her, if you dare.

Made in the USA
Charleston, SC
03 July 2014